SABRES IN THE SUN

SABRES IN THE SUN

Charles Whiting

CENTURY
LONDON SYDNEY AUCKLAND JOHANNESBURG

'What of the faith and fire within us,
Men who march away
Ere the barn-cocks say
Night is growing gray?'

THOMAS HARDY

Copyright © Charles Whiting 1991

All rights reserved

The right of Charles Whiting to be identified as the author of this
work has been asserted by him in accordance with the Copyright, Designs
and Patents Act 1988.

First published in Great Britain in 1991 by
Random Century Group
20 Vauxhall Bridge Road, London SW1V 2SA

Century Hutchinson South Africa (Pty) Ltd
PO Box 337, Bergvlei 2012, South Africa

Random Century Australia Pty Ltd
20 Alfred Street, Milsons Point, Sydney, NSW 2061
Australia

Random Century New Zealand Ltd
PO Box 40–086, Glenfield, Auckland 10
New Zealand

British Library Cataloguing in Publication Data
ISBN 0–7126–3048–1

Phototypeset by Input Typesetting Ltd, London
Printed in Great Britain by
Mackays of Chatham plc, Chatham, Kent

Preface

'After a short lull in Eastern warfare, the Burmese became elated by some recent conquests they had made. Being utterly ignorant of our power like all Orientals, towards the end of the year 1823 they were tempted to make sundry wanton attacks on us and our extending frontiers. Without notice given or any attempt to negotiate, they claimed possession of Shapuree – a little muddy isle in the province of Bengal, but close to the coast of the Arracan. Making a sudden night attack, they drove out a guard of British troops stationed there and, after killing several of them, took forcible possession of the whole place. As this event came close upon other outrages, retribution was necessary.

'Our Government summoned the Court of Ava to disavow participation in this affair, affecting to believe it the act of local authorities in the Arracan. The Burmese took this mildness as a proof of pusillanimity, boasting that the British Government of India dreaded entering into combat with them. They intimated plainly that unless their right to the island of Shapuree was distinctly admitted, the Victorious Lord of the White Elephant and the Golden Foot would invade the Company's dominions.'

Thus in that typical heavy-handed, mid-Victorian prose does Major General John Bold, V.C. begin his account of the First Burmese War. Here and in his latter writings about his life and career (*'Twixt Poona and Persia*, John Murray, 1863), Bold gives little indication of the key and dramatic rôle he himself played in the defeat of 'the Lord of the White Elephant and the Golden Foot'– as the ruler of Burma was so quaintly named. But by the time of writing, Bold was a very old and embittered man, obsessed with secrecy. Thanks, however, to the recent discovery (1988) of his personal papers and dispatches, we know a great deal more about his adventures in Burma and how he helped to add that country to the greatest empire the world had ever seen.

By 1823 when the war commenced, through no fault of his own Major John Bold had been exiled in India for nearly eight years. In that time he had founded 'Bold's Horse', the most famous of the native cavalry regiments of the East India Company's army, and had fought in half a score minor wars on the sub-continent.* Now for the first time since his disgrace at the Battle of Waterloo in 1815 he was to take part in a major campaign: the invasion and conquest of Burma.

Sabres in the Sun is the true story of Bold's amazing rôle in that invasion and conquest. It is a remarkable tale of how the small island nation of Britain, with few resources save its daring and imagination, could add yet another country – six times its own size – to its empire. It is not a pretty tale; but in those days when Britain was busy gobbling up one third of the world's surface for its own uses, there were few such. . . .

CHARLES WHITING, SPAIN, SUMMER 1990

* See *Bugles at Dawn* for further details of John Bold's early career and adventures.

ONE: CAPTURE!

1

The glare from the sun slashed the watchers' eyes like a sharp blade. It hung over the Bay of Bengal like a blood-red ball. Beneath it the blue wash of the sea was without a ripple. Not a breath of wind stirred. All was harsh, hot and threatening. There was impending danger in the very air.

Slowly Ensign Wallace of the Bengal Native Infantry lowered his spy-glass, his pale young face grim. 'There's no doubt about it then, sir,' he said. 'It's those murdering brown devils we've been hearing about these last months. They've come at last.'

Major John Bold, the commander of 'Bold's Horse', known throughout British India as 'Bold's Niggahs', did not reply at once. Instead he continued to gaze through his telescope at the line of junks for a few moments longer. They were outlined a stark black against the smooth expanse of water, every detail perfectly clear. They were no Burmese fishing junks, Bold could see that. Each of them mounted a brass two-pounder at the bows and he could make out the golden glint coming from the men's conical helmets. Those junks were manned by warriors all right and they were heading straight for this muddy mangrove swamp set in the Sea of Bengal and honoured by the name of Shapuree Island.

'I expect they are the Royal Invulnerables,' Wallace broke the brooding silence with a bitter laugh. 'They've been threatening to attack all autumn, though God only knows why they have picked on us here. The sacking of – er – Fort Shapuree is not exactly the same as taking Calcutta, is it, sir?'

Bold noted the mixture of bitterness and fear in the Ensign's voice and told himself Wallace was not yet eighteen. This would be his first action. Understandably he was scared, especially when the odds were so much against him and his handful of native sepoys. Finally Bold lowered his glass, his face lathered in sweat above the tight leather stock, and turned to the nervous youngster. Wallace saw just how set and determined that un-English face looked, with its jet-black curling side-whiskers. Suddenly he felt very confident. If anyone could see them through what was soon to come, it would be John Bold.

'There are roughly twenty men to a boat and there are ten boats,' Bold said in a matter-of-fact way like some village schoolmaster trying to example a simple arithmetic problem. 'That's two hundred against your thirty-odd native sepoys, Wallace.'

'We have the three-pounder, and my chaps are a stout bunch, sir,' Wallace said. 'Perhaps we can frighten them off with a show of force and a blast of grapeshot.'

Bold shook his head. 'From what I've heard of the Burmese, they attack when they're high on bhang, and that stuff is more potent than the grog we give to our fellers. It makes them think they can't be hit. No, we won't be able to frighten this little lot off, I'm afraid. We'll have to make a fight for it.'

Wallace swallowed hard and Bold allowed himself a smile, though his eyes remained as hard as ever. 'I know you are in command here, Wallace and I'm your guest. I *could* have picked a better place to spend a Christmas leave, could I not? No matter, if you prefer I can take over the defence.'

'It would please me greatly sir, if you would do me that honour,' Wallace replied hastily and there was no mistaking the note of relief in his voice.

Out over the water the war drums had commenced their solemn thunder. It would not be long now before the raiders started swarming ashore. 'Come on,' Bold urged Wallace as he grabbed his arm, 'let's get back to the fort.'

Together the two of them began to run across the stretch of damp sand towards the little wood-and-stone fort, built in the centre of the mud flats. Inside it, the black drummer boy was sounding an urgent call to arms, rattling away merrily on his kettle drum. Bold remembered the last time he had heard a drum beaten like that. It had been at Waterloo, eight years before, when little French drummer boys sounded what they called the *rappel* just before Old Boney's Imperial Guard came in for the last terrible blood bath. Now it was probably his turn to be slaughtered on this godforsaken island in the middle of nowhere.

The fort had been built in accordance with the ideas of the great French military engineer Vauban. Constructed round a small central stone citadel, it consisted of four star-shaped ramparts, made of stout timber. In theory, each point of the star could cover its neighbour with musket-fire. In practice Wallace simply did not have enough sepoys to man each position properly. So Bold told himself he would have to take a calculated risk; he would man only those portions of the ramparts directly under attack. The rest would have to be left to look after itself. 'Wallace!' he yelled, as the sepoys clambered up the ladders to their positions, 'you take charge of the three-pounder. As soon as the first junk comes in range, give it a burst of grape. We want to kill men, not sink ships. Is that clear?' There was iron in his voice now and suddenly Wallace felt a real soldier was in charge.

'Yessir,' the ensign sang out more cheerfully and doubled away to the central point of the star, where the half-naked gunners were already poised over their cannon.

Bold drew his sabre and flung a glance at the sepoys with their dark glistening faces. They would be stout chaps, he told himself, as long as they stuck together and followed orders. One break in discipline and they'd run. He raised his voice above the boom of the war drums, 'Listen to me, soldiers,' he said in their own tongue. 'I am Bold of Bold's Horse. You have all heard of me. I have commanded soldiers of your race ever since I first came to India and beaten both brown men and white. Now *we* shall fight and beat those yellow men from over the sea,' he indicated the junks with a sweep of his sabre. But to do so, we need *discipline*! There will be no individual firing, but just a concentrated volley when I give the command – not before.' He raised his sabre, the blade flashing silver in the sun. 'Take aim!'

Everywhere the sepoys raised their heavy muskets and dug the butts hard into their skinny shoulders, their faces set and determined. Bold nodded his approval. They wouldn't let him down. Silently he counted off the distance. *Two hundred yards . . . one hundred and fifty . . . one hundred yards. . . .* Soon the lead junk would be within range of Wallace's three-pounder and already the head gunner had his slow match burning, poised over the barrel, while his assistants stood ready with pail, ram and powder kegs . . . *Seventy-five yards.* . . . 'Mister Wallace,' Bold barked.

'Yessir,' Wallace called back, feeling a thin trickle of sweat course unpleasantly down the small of his back. In a minute the yellow rogues would be landing on the mud flat, if they weren't stopped.

'Prepare to fire!'

'Sir!'

Without waiting to be ordered in his own tongue, the half-naked gunner held his slow match close to the hole, a nerve ticking frantically at his temple. Bold opened his mouth again. He was totally in control of himself, yet he seemed to hear and see everything more acutely than was customary: the soft slap of the water on the mud flats; the slow hiss of the match; the whitened knuckles of the sepoys as they took first pressure and the nervous breathing of the little drummer boy. Bold counted to three, then he yelled at the top of his voice, 'FIRE!'

The gunner dropped his match to the hole. A flash of violent light. A cloud of black smoke. And with a great roar the cannon leapt back on its four wheels like a wild horse being put to the reins for the first time. Suddenly the black grape was hurtling flatly across the blue wash of the sea, heading for the lead junk.

Bold tensed for the impact, the palm gripping his sabre suddenly wet with warm sweat. Pray God, the gunner would hit the craft. Metal struck wood. The junk came

6

to an abrupt halt, its mast tumbling down with a vicious rending of wood. At the same time the raiders in the junk were galvanised into crazy action. Leaping, falling, clawing at each other in their urgency, they started to drop everywhere, as legs, arms, heads were ripped off and the junk was turned into a mad charnel house; the blood of the massed dead and dying, packed tightly together in that death ship, already seeping through its timbers to stain the water outside a pale pink.

Wallace whooped with excitement, waving his shako wildly in the air as the shattered junk, with its cargo of death, started to drift erractically.

'Reload, Mister Wallace!' Bold cried, seeing the other junks alter course to avoid the stricken craft, for they knew it would be their turn next otherwise.

Sweating frantically, the gunners sluiced their cannon, rammed fresh gunpowder down the muzzle, followed by grape, yelping with pain whenever they inadvertently touched the dull-glowing purple barrel. 'Ready,' Wallace yelled. 'FIRE!' Again the cannon thundered. But obviously the gunner was rattled, for already the second junk in line had altered course, its men plunging over the sides, ready to take their chances in the shallow water. The burst of grape missed by a dozen yards, raising huge spouts of churning white water, but doing no harm whatsoever. He had missed!

Bold cursed and then forgot the gunner. The first of the raiders, helmets gleaming in the sun, were already splashing through the shallows towards the mud flats. 'Hold your fire, you sepoys . . . till they're in the mud,' Bold yelled in warning, 'Stand fast now!'

The sepoys relaxed a little. They understood. Once the raiders were floundering in the thigh-deep mud, they would make easier targets. But they reasoned, too, that Bold Sahib was taking a risk. Once the raiders were ashore in force, there'd be little to stop them. As Wallace's cannon thundered once more, another junk reeled as if struck by a sudden storm. Its sail came crashing down, sweeping screaming men overboard with it. In that same instant the first of the raiders hit the oozing green mud. At once they began to flounder knee deep in the stinking goo, waving their weapons impotently above their heads, trying to maintain their balance. Bold waited no longer. They were the perfect target – sitting ducks the lot of them. 'FIRE!' he commanded and flashed his silver sabre above his bare head.

The sepoys fired with a will, the tension broken at last. A crackle of angry blue flame ran the length of their positions on the rampart. Black smoke erupted from a score or so muskets. For a moment it veiled the scene below, but the sudden wild screams of agony told Bold they hadn't missed with that first tremendous salvo. The smoke cleared to reveal men writhing in the mud on all sides, flailing their arms in their desperate attempts to fight off death, or struggling to reach their feet again, depending how they'd fared. For a moment Bold simply stood there, sensing the shock of the young sepoys at the sight of the havoc their volley had created. But there was no time to dwell on the awesome beauty of a battle-field; he had seen it often enough in the past. 'Reload!' he commanded and pulled out his own pistol.

Bold let the sepoys wait for the next order; there was no use wasting ammunition and it was obvious they had won the first round. The junks were hesitant now, slowly moving out of range of Wallace's three-pounder, while the survivors of that first rush to the mud-flats were burying themselves even deeper into the thick clinging goo, as if digging their own graves. Bold wiped the dripping sweat from his brow and tried to out-think the raiders. For already some of the junks had slipped behind the cover of the bamboo which grew thickly at the edge of the swamp. Where were they heading? Where would they attempt to attack his perimeter? Dammit, if only he knew *now* how to make his dispositions! Out at sea the blood-red ball of the sun had started to slip down towards the far horizon. Now some of the junks were anchored well out of cannonshot reach, no sign of life on their decks, while the others remained vanished behind the bamboo.

8

Every second sepoy had stood down to rest in whatever shade could be found on the ramparts, while the others, sun-flap spread behind their shakos, peered out at the limitless sea.

Wallace licked his parched lips. Bold had already rationed the Fort's limited water to one pannikin per man per every three hours. 'What do you think, Major?'

Bold gave a weary smile, for it was now four hours since the first attack and he was getting tired of standing on the ramparts, waiting for them to come again. 'Well, there are three alternatives,' he lectured the younger man, 'the *badmash*,' he meant villians, 'can go away and leave us in peace which is, I think, highly unlikely. They can try a frontal assault over the mud flats. Again, in my opinion, not on the cards. Or,' Bold paused significantly, 'they can do what every commander with superiority of numbers and flexibility of movement would do.'

'And what is that, sir?' Wallace inquired innocently.

'Why, Wallace, wait till darkness and then come at us from two directions – and all directions for that matter. For they know by now that we haven't got sufficient strength to man every rampart.'

Wallace pondered for a moment, then said, 'What do you think then, sir?'

'This, Wallace, I think we'd better get a work detail chopping up some of Fort Shapuree. We want plenty of firewood for this coming night. Then once that is done, I want most of your sepoys to retire to the citadel,' Bold indicated the stone tower which dominated the centre of the compound. 'I shall remain behind with the gunners and – say half a dozen sepoys to man the three-pounder.'

'But why, sir?' a puzzled Wallace asked.

When Bold hastily explained his plan. Wallace frowned. 'Risky, sir,' he opined. 'If it doesn't work, well, sir,' he hesitated, face blushing, 'we'll lose the cannon . . . and er, you're for the chop, sir.'

Bold looked down at him, as somewhere behind the mangroves the war drums commenced their insidious

booming. 'Yes, Wallace,' he said with a note of weariness,'
John Bold Esquire has been – er – *for the chop* since the
day he was born. . . . '

2

The war drums thundered: steady, persistent and threatening. A couple of times the defenders ringed in by their fires thought they seemed to be coming closer. Then they would rouse themselves from lethargy and grab their weapons, hearts suddenly beating like trip-hammers. Others would hurriedly thrust fresh brands on the circle of fires so that the flames leapt higher, and peer suspiciously into the dark mass of the mangroves. But each time was a false alarm, a trick played on the nervous sepoys by the changing night breeze from the sea.

It was now four o'clock on the morning of December 26th, 1823 and a weary Bold lay slumped next to the three-pounder. He told himself that on the other side of the world the good people of England would be celebrating the end of another Christmas. All those middle class burghers, prosperous on the money they made from their John Company shares, would be dancing the last 'Roger de Coverley' and toasting each other in a midnight cup of mulled port. There'd be snow outside and a chill wind, with a good log fire crackling in the big hearth. All would be heartiness and good cheer. Here, however, on this dismal stretch of mud flat, a scared white boy masquerading as an officer in the army of the East India Company and a soured major of native cavalry were probably about to breathe their last in order to protect those precious shares. Bold yawned lazily and told himself it did not really matter. Nothing mattered much, when you considered it. For a white man life was short and brutal in India anyway. If the fever didn't carry him off, some native assassin would. The only thing that really counted was to die as a man, with pride and honour.

Suddenly his amateur philosophizing came to an abrupt halt. Good soldier that he was, he was totally aware, and

11

cocked his head to one side to listen. Yes, there it was again! A slithering sound like that a big snake makes through wet sand. And something else too. The muted creaking of ropes. There were men out there and they were dragging something with them. Tapping his boot automatically to check that his pistol was still in position, Bold placed his hand over the mouth of the head gunner so that he wouldn't cry out in alarm and whispered in his ear, 'Light the slow match – at once!' Without waiting to see that his order was being carried out, he scurried round his little command, nudging each sepoy into wakefulness before running, crouched almost double, to the door of the citadel. With the hilt of his sabre he gave three sharp knocks in the signal he had agreed upon with Wallace. It meant *stand to*; *they're coming*. A minute later he was back with the men, who had automatically formed two lines to each side of the three-pounder, the front rank kneeling bayonets fixed, the rear rank standing. Bold nodded in approval. Wallace's sepoys were good men. He could rely on them. So they waited, tension increasing by the moment. And there came a new noise, quite a way off, but distinct enough. It reached the rear of the citadel. Whatever the Burmese were up to, Bold told himself, they were doing so from two sides. He frowned. Things were becoming very difficult. Despite the first pink flush of dawn, the sun wouldn't appear for another half an hour yet and their fires were burning down. Bold daren't risk breaking his line in order to have the sepoys put more wood on them. The result was that the circle of surrounding shadows was becoming ever darker. Around him Bold could hear the heavy breathing of his sepoys. One of them began to hawk throatily before spitting in the loud Indian fashion and the gunner hissed, 'Hold they wind, prick of a pig!' The sepoy closed his mouth hurriedly.

Now there was no mistaking the sounds all around them in the mangroves. The swamps were full of men. The Burmese were coming in force, Bold knew that. What the devil were those slithering noises? The next minute he had his answer. Scarlet flame stabbed the darkness. Boom!

Two black objects, chained together, came hurtling straight at his little force. 'DUCK!' Bold yelled frantically and did so himself in the very same moment that the first burst of chainshot came hissing over their bent heads to slam against the stone wall of the tower. 'God blast their eyes!' Bold yelled at no one in particular as he realised what the Burmese had done. During the night they had dismantled the swivel guns from the bows of the junks and hauled them ashore and then through the jungle until they were close enough to be in firing range. Now they would subject his little force to a fine old barrage before they charged.

He swung round on the gunner, already crouched there over the barrel with his glowing slow match. 'Load cannister,' he yelled as the swivel gun thundered once more. 'Cannister – quick, man!' In his excitement he spoke in English, not the native tongue. But the gunner understood the word 'cannister' all right – a collection of ball and fragments of iron, deadly at close range. In turn he rapped out an order in his own language and with frantic fingers his assistants reloaded and waited. Bold raised his hand, pistol already clenched in his left fist. 'Prepare to fire!' he cried above the thunder of the swivels booming on all sides now, their shot slamming into the stone walls of the citadel and gouging great chunks of masonry from them. Bold hesitated one more moment and then there they were, high on bhang, yelling their heads off, whirling their weapons in triumph, as they came bursting out of the mangroves, scores of them. 'FIRE!' he shrieked.

The three-pounder flashed. The cannister sped straight towards the running men. Bold did not wait for the deadly shell to strike. Instead he ordered, 'Front rank – FIRE!' The sepoys did not hesitate. The tension was broken at last. As one they pressed their triggers in the same moment that the cannister exploded just to the front of the attackers. A sharp crack. A sheet of violet flame and jagged, first-sized shards of metal were flying everywhere.

The Burmese stopped as if they had just run into an invisible wall. Men dropped screaming and howling everywhere, great wounds ripped their flesh, from amidst a mess of flailing arms and legs a severed head came rolling over the wet sand like a football abandoned by some careless schoolboy. A second later, the survivors had fled back the way they had come. The second Burmese attack on Fort Shapuree had failed. . . .

Dawn. The weary defenders slumped full-length on the ground, their faces hollowed out to scarlet death-heads by the rising sun, as the cannon still continued to pound away. Five minutes before, Wallace's men on the citadel ramparts had managed to lower down a few canteens of tepid water and a handful of cold chapattis for the sepoys. But all of them craved more, feeling their thirst grow as the sun rose. It was going to be another searingly hot December day, thought Bold, crouching next to the gunner, wondered idly whether any one of them would ever see the end of it. It was only a matter of time now before the Burmese rushed them again. He could already smell the sickly sweet odour of bhang wafting from their hiding places in the mangroves and knew they were working themselves up once more with the drug. The drums had begun beating once more, too. It wouldn't be long now.

Above him Wallace croaked – for they, too, were deadly short of water – Major . . . Major Bold, sir.'

'Yes?'

'More junks, sir . . . about ten of them coming in from the south.'

Bold groaned softly. That might well mean another two hundred Burmese warriors when they were hopelessly outnumbered already. But he did not show his dismay to young Wallace. Instead he called back, 'Perhaps they're heading elsewhere.' Then he put more confidence into his voice than he felt and added, 'Standfast, young Wallace, we're not finished yet by a long chalk!'

As time passed leadenly, Bold desperately racked his brains for some way out. For a little while he considered a defiant last charge, risking everything in attempting to break through to the anchored junks and escape in that manner. But when his eyes fell on the Burmese sprawled out in the extravagant postures of the violently-done-to-death, the flies already buzzing around their unseeing faces, the vultures hovering overhead in the burning air, he abandoned the idea. The Burmese hidden in the mangroves would mow them down before they had gone twenty yards. There was the citadel, of course. By carefully rationing their water they might hold out inside it for a couple of days. But what then? The next supply brig from Calcutta was not expected for another fortnight – it was to be the same ship which would have taken him back to his own unit, Bold's Horse, patrolling the Aracan. They'd never last another fourteen days without water. So what was the alternative? The increasing fury of the Burmese war drums told him that there was none. Here they would have to stand and die. They were in for another attack.

This time the Burmese forces planned better. The first salvo of their guns was not aimed indiscriminately like last time. Now they discharged a first volley at both the top of the citadel and Bold's three-pounder. And they were lucky. That furious burst of grapeshot sliced lethally through the air and caught the three-pounder's crew just as they were hunched around their weapon preparing to fire cannister. They reeled back in all directions, screaming with pain. '*Standfast sepoys!*' Bold yelled urgently and sprang to the aid of the chief gunner. It was no use. As the man writhed back and forth on the ground, the slow match still gripped in his skinny brown hand, Bold recoiled with horror. Where the gunner's eyes had once been there were two purple pits, empty and suppurating. But there was no time to concern himself with that now. Already their enemies were streaming forward, high on bhang again, yelling their heads off, as their swords flashed silver in the sun.

'First rank – 'FIRE!' Bold cried. The volley rang out, smacking directly into the leading Burmese. The front runners went down as if pole-axed. Bold had no time for the agonies of the attackers as they experienced the throes

15

of death. While his first rank reloaded madly, knowing that they'd be overrun at any minute now, he cried, 'Second rank – FIRE!' Again a murderous salvo rang out. Again a dozen or so of the attackers hit the ground, writhing and twisting in their mortal agony. But there was no stopping them any more. They were far too many and now they came in screaming for the kill.

The sepoys raised their long steel bayonets. Bold fired without aiming. At that range he couldn't miss. A Burmese was hit in the face. It disintegrated, his features slipping down the gleaming bones of the skull like red molten wax. But still they kept on coming – and then they were in among the sepoys. A wild crazy mêlée commenced in which men swayed back and forth, grunting like animals, mouthing terrible obscenities, each isolated in his own cocoon of fear. They stabbed, they parried, lunged, thrust, chopped: animals all carried away by the mad unreasoning, atavistic fury of battle. Men went down screaming underfoot to be trampled on unfeelingly by their comrades. Other men staggered out of the conflict exhibiting their wounds to anyone who might wish to see, their eyes wild and wide in utter disbelief that this could be happening to them.

A Burmese raider dashed at Bold. His bare feet kicked up the dust so that he appeared to be running through a little white cloud. In his upraised hand he held a gleaming cleaver twice the size of a butcher's chopper back home. His yellow-brown face dripped with sweat and his dark eyes were wild and unfocused like those of a wild animal. It was obvious that he was on drugs. Red, betel-stained teeth bared, gasping for breath, he aimed a tremendous blow at Bold's skull. At the very last moment, Bold parried with his sabre. There was the ringing clash of metal. Bold felt the shock of impact run right up his arm. Desperately he slipped out his own blade from beneath the cleaver. The Burmese danced clear, knowing instinctively what was coming. Again Bold tried. He had not the time for the fancy tactics of a French fencing master. The Burmese were swarming all around him. Instead of raising

16

the sabre above his head to bring it down on the opponent's skull in the traditional manner, he unleashed a tremendous side-swipe at the Burmese's naked ribs. It caught the man completely off guard. The blade went through his ribs like a hot knife through butter as he screamed shrilly like a woman. When he dropped to his knees, chopper falling from suddenly nerveless fingers, blood jetted from his side in a bright scarlet spurt. For a moment or so the two of them – the victor and the vanquished – poised there, as if frozen in some ghastly tableau for eternity. Then Bold, realising his danger, levered his right foot against the dying man's chest and pulled the blade out with a dreadful sucking noise. Next instant the Burmese pitched face forward into the dust, dead before he hit the ground.

Now Bold was retreating to the citadel with the surviving sepoys, while Wallace's men kept up a ragged fire above, which was becoming weaker by the second. Out of the corner of his eye, Bold – his sabre flashing to left and right as he carved a path for himself – saw a sepoy go down to his knees, drop his musket and raise his hands in the classic pose of supplication, as if he were appealing to some god on high for mercy. But on this December day, in the season of goodwill to all men, his god was looking the other way. In a flash he was surrounded by yelling, drug-crazed Burmese, who started to hack and thrust, ripping great red gouges of flesh out of his defenceless body until thankfully he fell dead at their naked feet. Then it was Bold's turn. He felt a great blow at the side of his head. His shako tumbled to the dust and he felt himself overwhelmed by a sense of nausea. He shook his head desperately, trying to fight off the black cloud which threatened to engulf him. He faltered and stood there swaying. Yet he tried to go on, the sabre held weakly in his hand, thrusting pain in his side. Like a red-hot poker being skewered through his flesh. He felt himself scream with the electric agony of it. All was blurred . . . The ground seemed to rise to meet him and then fall back like a wave crashing on a beach . . . The sabre fell from a limp hand. . . .

'No, Major Bold, you must not try,' he thought he heard a voice say in English. And his legs were giving way beneath him, as if they were made of jelly . . . Wallace was dragged out, screaming . . . They were doing something to his hand with a hammer and nail. Then the screaming disappeared into the distance . . . He was going down a tunnel . . . He fought it frantically.

'NO . . . NO . . . NO . . . !' He hit the ground hard. His mouth flooded with a hot coppery-tasting liquid. Blood spurted from his nostrils. He gave one last groan. Then nothing.

3

'Gentlemen, the Governor-General,' the flunkey announced and the assembled officers and officials of the East India Company rose obediently to their feet, as outside the thunder rumbled and the noon sky darkened. They were in for a storm, they told themselves, as Lord Amherst entered the big assembly room in his usual pompous and overbearing manner. He was a short, stocky man with a large nose and cleft chin, a sure sign of pig-headedness. Now he passed down the line of waiting men, nodding to some, bowing to others.

'You'd think yon men was bluidy king o' England himsen,' General Archibald Campbell, the senior officer present, whispered to his aide. 'Will ye look at the way the mon struts!'

Completing his progress the Governor-General ascended the raised dias and seated himself at his throne-like chair. 'Gentlemen,' he announced even before they had taken their seats again, 'I have had enough!' He mopped his brow and in the side room, the punkah wallahs agitated the roof fans more energetically – for a few moments. 'I simply have had enough of those damned Burmese over there,' he indicated east. For months they have been raiding our frontiers. Last month four or five thousand of those yellow rogues even had the audacity to march within two hundred miles of us here in Calcutta and entrench themselves at Sylhet. It took the loss of one hundred of our stout fellows under Major Newton,' he nodded to a tall young officer, his head still bandaged from the wound he had received at Sylhet, 'to drive them out again. That done with, what did the yellow devils do then?' He flushed with anger, while outside the thunder rolled across the leaden sky threateningly, 'Why they attacked again and got within a thousand yards of our positions at Bhadrapour. Once more they had to be driven off with considerable loss of life. Now, gentlemen, my latest intelligence this morning is that they have had the absolutely unprecedented impertinence to capture Shapuree Island and massacre our whole garrison there!' His jowls shook with rage.

'Highland Archie', as General Campbell was known behind his back – no one would have dared to use that nickname to his face – frowned. 'That means that yon braw laddie, Major Bold, is lost as weel, sir,' he commented. 'I sent him personally to the island to make a reconnaissance. The murdering yeller devils!' The General tugged his bulbous and pitted red nose, the product of several decades of imbibing his native land's favourite tipple, 'A sad loss . . . a verry sad loss.'

'Yes, yes,' the Governor-General said hastily. 'Now General, will you please let me proceed. Time is urgent. Now with the news of the loss of Shapuree Island, we have had further alarming intelligence. It is that one of these Burmese leaders, a certain Maha Bandoola,' he pronounced the name, as if he had just tasted something very unpleasant, 'who apparently is in great favour with their court at Rangoon, is assembling a great army to march north. From there he will attack our positions on the Arracan and follow that by seizing our own province of Bengal. The rogue has even declared publicly that he will bring with him a set of golden fetters. These will be used to imprison *me* and drag me back to their own capital, Rangoon, like some damned Roman slave. There I am to be flung in front of their ruler the Lord of – dashit, Weston, what the devil is the heathen's outlandish title?'

Weston, the Governor-General's constantly harassed military secretary, supplied the Burmese ruler's title hastily, 'the Lord of the White Elephant and the Golden Foot, my lord,' he said.

'Yes, that's it, Amherst snorted. 'Whatever that damned gibberish can possibly mean!'

General Campbell smiled softly at the sight of the pompous Governor's red-faced indignation, and stroking his

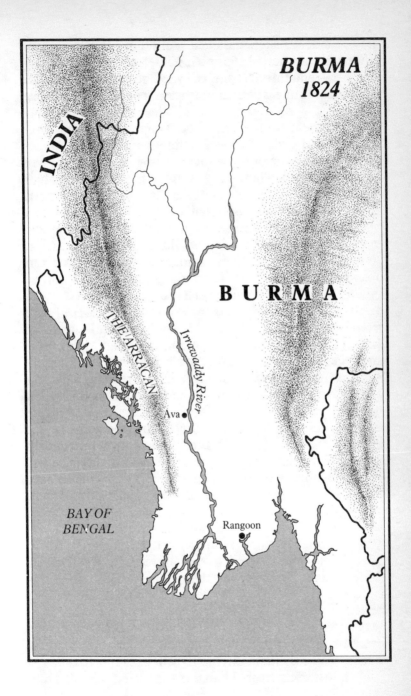

BURMA
1824

INDIA

BURMA

THE ARRACAN

Irrawaddy River

Ava ●

BAY OF
BENGAL

Rangoon
●

greying side whiskers indulged himself in a mental picture of a naked Amherst laden with golden chains being dragged bare-foot through the crowded streets of Rangoon. That would take down the arrogant wee little man a peg or two!

'Now then, gentlemen,' the Governor-General continued, raising his voice against the storm outside, 'we of the Company cannot allow those yellow devils to continue their raiding any longer. A stop must be put to their ambitions on our territory once and for all. Now Weston, will you explain the basic plan.'

Weston, who was possessed of one of those dry yellow faces typical of those who would die young in India, rose to his feet quickly. He said: 'Your lordship, we can assemble a force of some six thousand foot, basically native infantry, but with white artillery and my Lord Cavendish's 42nd Foot, which is being currently disembarked here from England.' He nodded to the young officer lounging at one of the windows, puffing at a cheroot and toying with an eyeglass as if totally bored by all this provincial chatter.

Lord Amherst beamed at Cavendish, for he was the son of his own younger brother. General Campbell, for his part, frowned at the young fop in his London-made regimentals, heavy with gold braid. Why the fellow was hardly thirty and already he was a Lieutenant Colonel. Probably another of those useless aristocrats whose fathers had bought them a regiment in order to be rid of them before they were involved in some London society scandal or other. The British Army was full of such useless creatures, he told himself and tugged angrily at his nose.

'This army,' Weston went on, 'will be commanded by General Campbell, whom as you all know is a veteran of the Peninsula Wars against Old Boney.' He flashed the big Scot, who wore a thick heavy kilt despite the stifling heat, a careful smile. 'If I may be so bold as to say so – a very able soldier indeed.' There was a murmur of agreement from the assembled company. Hardened veteran that he was 'Highland Archie' blushed. He looked down at his big shining boots like an embarrassed schoolboy.

The Governor-General said somewhat impatiently: 'Get on with it, man!'

'Well, gentlemen, the Govenor-General in his wisdom,' the military secretary continued, 'has decided that our army will avoid the barran mountains of the Arracan and the pestilential jungles of the Chittagong. Instead we shall attack the heart of their empire itself – *Rangoon!*'

There was a gasp of surprise from the notables, as outside lightning zig-zagged the sky in dramatic fury. Voices rose with urgent questions on all sides. *'But milord, the length of our supply lines . . . what of the necessary shipping from Calcutta . . . How can we protect ourselves with the enemy on both banks of the water approach to Rangoon?'* And all the while Lord Cavendish gawped through his eyeglass attached by a silken cord to his neck, a silly smile on his rather horsey face as if it were all one great joke.

Lord Amherst, pleased with the surprise he had achieved with his bold plan, raised his hands for silence and when the assembly had quietened down, said, 'Perhaps, at this juncture I should let General Campbell have his say. After all he is going to execute the plan in the end.'

'Yes, yes,' several agreed, 'Let Old Highland Archie tell us how *he's* going to make sense of such an outlandish idea.' The General glowered as he overheard the use of the nickname which he disliked intensely, took a pinch of snuff to clear his head, gave an enormous sneeze into a yellow-stained handkerchief and then stepped into the centre of the assembly hall, his kilt swinging above his brawny calves.

At the window Lord Cavendish sniggered and said, 'Oh, I say, not one of those highlanders. By Gad, haven't you India johnnies anything better than that to lead us?' The Governor-General shot his nephew a hard look and the foppish young Colonel shut up, but the disrespectful grin did not disappear from his face.

'Ye knew, the lot of ye, that I'm no much of a speakin' mon, Campbell commenced.' 'I'm a sodjer, have been since I was a wee laddie, fresh weaned from my mother's tit – not like some.' He gave Lord Cavendish a fierce glance and those who did not depend upon the Governor-General's patronage laughed, knowing exactly what the big Scot meant. 'Weel, gentlemen, I'll put to ye like this,' he said. 'If we took – ye ken – the logical route across yon country, I swear I'd be a general without an army by the time I reached Rangoon. The fever and the country would feckle my laddies – black and white. They'd die like flies.' He paused to let his words sink in then said, 'So the consequence is that we'll have to take risks.' He nodded to the military secretary and as arranged beforehand, Weston unrolled a great chart of the Sea of Bengal and Burma and pinned it to the opposite wall for all to see. 'My plan is to asemble two divisions,' Campbell continued, while his audience craned their necks to see the chart. Outside the rain was beginning to come down in earnest. 'One from Calcutta here and the other from Madras. They will meet at Fort Cornwallis on the Andaman Isles. Each division will be carried by troopers and in the case of our own Bengal Division, the men will be protected not only by His Majesty's ships *Lifey* and *Larne* but also by one of yon newfangled steam vessels, *HMS Diana*.

There were exclamations of surprise from his listeners. Even Lord Cavendish looked suddenly attentive. The Governor-General, they reasoned, must be taking the operation very seriously if he were prepared to risk one of Britain's latest inventions in the undertaking. Indeed, there could not be more than half a dozen steamships in the whole of the sub-continent.

'From the islands, the General continued, 'we sail to the mouth of the Irrawaddy and thence to Rangoon itself. I would venture a guess that the whole passage will take no more than five to six days.'

'All well and good, General,' Lord Cavendish said in a high-pitched sneering voice which grated immediately on the Scot, 'but what do you know of the defences of Rangoon and the portability of the river itself? Indeed all I know of the place is what I recall from reading Marco

Polo back at Eton and if my beak there was right, that particular Venetian gentleman wrote his *Travels* some several centuries ago. Pray General Campbell, what do you say to that?'

The Scot's slab-like face flushed a dangerous red. He calmed himself with difficulty. After all, it was the same objection he had made himself when the Governor-General had first discussed the armed expedition with him. 'Why, your Excellency,' he had protested, 'it would be a venture into the unknown, like sailing to the centre of darkest Africa if that were possible. We know nothing of yon country beyond the water. Ye know, we'd be like a blindfolded prize-fighter punching away in a dark cellar!'

The Governor-General had not been able to quell his overwhelming doubts, but since then General Campbell had had time to think about it and come up with a reply. 'Lord Cavendish,' he said with an irritated rasp to his voice which would have made more sensitive men than Cavendish beware, 'as I have already said, I'd be a general without an army if I attempted to take the land route. So I will venture into the virtual unknown, basing my hopes of success on the fact that those yellow Burmese heathens will not expect such a bold stroke.' He stared at the foppish Englishman with his fancy regalia, 'Indeed I'll wager ye a hundred guineas here and now that when we anchor off Rangoon, we'll catch those rogues completely by surprise.'

Lord Cavendish sniffed. 'My dear General,' he answered, face set in a supercilious expression, as he again toyed with his absurd lorgnette, 'I am not accustomed to accept wagers which I know in advance I shall win. I do not consider that sporting.'

With thirty-odd years of military authority in his voice Campbell barked, 'Well, milord, if ye are so confident that the expedition to Rangoon will fail, will you and your regiment refuse to accompany it?' He stared hard at the fop.

Suddenly all eyes were turned in Cavendish's direction

25

and he blushed, his weak chin trembling slightly. 'I never said anything about not. . . . '

'Come on, sir,' Campbell insisted. 'Are you prepared to fight or not? Out with it.'

'General Campbell,' the Governor-General almost shouted, rising from his throne-like chair. 'My nephew Lord Cavendish might not like the plan, but he knows his duty. Whatever the difficulties ahead he will not deflect from carrying out the orders of his superiors. You may rest assured of that.'

Campbell went a beetroot colour, his ham-like fists clenched in impotent rage. It was always the same. These aristocratic swells always landed on their feet. They won not because they had talent and experience, but because they had money and power. Cavendish was a craven coward, he could see that now. But he would end his days, dying in bed, heaped with his country's honours and decorations. While he, old 'Highland Archie' as he knew they called him behind his back, would be mouldering in some pauper's grave or dead on some obscure battlefield, unhonoured and unsung. Then he relaxed with a sigh. It had always been that way in England and it always would be. Nothing he could do would change it. 'Gentlemen,' he said quietly as Cavendish raised his eye-glass once more and quizzed Campbell as if he were a particularly comic form of life, 'there is much to be done and I expect every one of you concerned with this venture to report to me on the fitness of your undertakings by the end of the week. 'Milord,' he turned to the Governor-General.

Amherst surveyed the Scot for a moment and told himself that young Cavendish was a damned silly fool if he rubbed Campbell up any more. The Scot would ensure that there was no glory and no easy pickings in the form of loot for him, if he didn't watch his step. He'd have to have a word with Cavendish later. Now he said in a solemn tone, 'Gentlemen, this is a great undertaking that we are about. Not only for the East India Company but for the glory of the Old Country. We are committed not just to the punishment of those yellow devils on the other side of the sea. We are also committed to adding yet another country to our empire. From now onwards history will be gazing down on each and every one of us.'

General Campbell raised his right leg and gave a malicious great fart but it went unheard. For in that same instant the storm gathered all its fury and the rain came pelting down in one solid sheet of icy grey. The assembly was over.

4

At times the glare and heat of the burning tropical sun would rouse him momentarily from his state of blessed unconsciousness, making him toss and turn in misery. Or the gust and howl of a sudden typhoon racing across the Bay of Bengal from the south-west, followed by a hail of hot rain to sluice his fevered frame, would stir him long enough to lick his scummed lips and ease his raging thirst. But mostly the soft rythmic to and fro of the swaying junk bearing him back to the homeland of the murderers lulled him back into the benison of sleep and the dreams which came with that blessed state.

There would be Waterloo. Always Waterloo. It had been his first experience of battle as a boy. It had been the start, too, of his disgrace, the quarrel and that last interview with his lordship, the Duke of Wellington, the victor of Waterloo, which had sent him into exile for ever. In that direct Irish manner of his the Duke had snapped, 'You blotted your copy book because you felt you were doing the right thing, Bold. Unfortunately you do not know the ways of the rich and powerful. For that you must pay the price of youthful stupidity. Nevertheless you have my best wishes for the future. Good luck to you in India, John Bold. And now I must piss . . . '

In his tortured dreams as the crowded junk tossed and pitched in the waves, John Bold relived the adventures and dangers of his passage to India up to that day when the old Governor-General Hastings had given him the command of a half-squadron of raw Indian recruits to turn into Bold's Horse. 'Bold's Niggahs' had done a thousand times better than anyone in Calcutta had expected. From the day they had crossed the River Nag on January 7th, 1816 they had carved their path across half of India, breaking the power of the Pindaree princes and adding another handsome chunk of native Indian territory to the ever growing empire of the British East India Company. But his own success had been soured by bitter disappointment. The girl he had loved so dearly had married another: that same aristocrat who had run away at Waterloo, had attempted to murder him thereafter in order to achieve revenge and had finally done just that by using his money and position to marry Bold's beloved Georgina. All his life seemed to have been like that – military success hand in hand with private failure.

Yet as the junk bore him ever closer to the mysterious kingdom of the Lord of the White Elephant and the Golden Foot, John Bold's fevered mind pictured again the kindly old face of Hastings looking like a bald monkey, but infinitely wise, as he told him, 'You will go far in the Company's service, young Bold. *Destiny has put its mark on you.* Disappointments you will undoubtedly suffer. But always remember this my boy, however much adversity tries to lay you low, you will survive and rise above it to greatness.' In moments of clarity between his bouts of fever he wondered at the truth of Hastings' words.

The rest of the garrison of the doomed island of Shapuree had been slaughtered. God knows how terrible those last moments of poor young Wallace had been! They had nailed him to the door of the citadel, hammering big gleaming nails through his wrists and feet in an obscene parody of the ordeal of Our Lord. But they had added one final indignity to the torture of the young ensign by slicing off his penis and thrusting it into his mouth to look as if he had choked to death on his own organ.

Yet John Bold had been allowed to live. He reasoned they must have brought him water, even food, as he lay here drifting in and out of unconsciousness in the scuppers of the junk. It must have been about five days after he had been taken that the fever finally left him and it was then that he realized he could smell land. There was no denying it. Most of the time on the junk his nostrils had been assailed during his waking moments by the smell of his captors – garlic, peppers, the oil they used on their skins, sweat. Now on the freshening breeze, he could detect the familiar reek of the East. They were slowly making a landfall. But where? When he managed to raise his head over the rail, he caught a glimpse of a splindly-looking structure on four legs a couple of miles away and the faint brown of a coast. It was a lighthouse and he suspected it must mean they were approaching an important area like Rangoon. By supporting himself painfully on one elbow he could see that the coast was inhabited and prosperous. There were villages everywhere, clusters of palm-leaf canopies huddled close to the white sands upon which rested row after row of fishing sampans. Smoke curled lazily into the blue sky on all sides and once he caught a faint glimpse of happy naked children splashing in the white curve of the surf. By the late afternoon the villages seemed to have grown bigger and he sensed somehow that they were slowly reaching their destination.

Twilight came. On shore hundreds of tiny palm-oil lights flickered bravely against the coming darkness. The junk was now gliding down a muddy estuary, the leadsman on the bow swinging his weighted line and calling out the soundings as they went along. Somehow the sight and the slow pace of their progress soothed Bold. His apprehensions about the future vanished and, veteran soldier that he was, he set about collecting as much visual information as he could about the land of his enemies, storing it for the future. It was about then he saw it. At first it was merely a glint of golden light reflected beyond the trees. The palms swept back and he gasped at the full beauty of what was now revealed: not a single building, but a collection clinging to the hillside which dominated the sprawling town beyond: a fairytale palace like those of the stories he had read as an infant. Building after building, each roofed in gold, and crowning all in the centre was a great dome of burnished gold. 'Like a big yellow tit,' General Campbell would characterize it weeks later in that prosaic, no-nonsense manner of his. But now John Bold, wounded and captive, gazed upon it in awe,

30

as if he might well be entering paradise itself. '*The Golden Pagoda of Rangoon!*' he breathed.

One day later John Bold lay on a silken couch, his body bathed and lotioned, his wounds tended. He was toying with a bowl or rice and cinnamon stems. Next to it lay another bowl of tender turtle flesh, wrapped in mango leaves. The food had been served with great ceremony by young Burmese women, whose small and firm rose-tipped breasts peeped invitingly through the white cotton tops they wore. But on this second day of January, 1824 John Bold was not very interested in either the food or the breasts of the obliging Burmese servants. As he lay there listening to the boom of the gongs from the Golden Pagoda and the cries of the peacocks and monkeys far below in the ornamental garden, he wondered not only why he had been spared, but also why he was being housed in such luxury. 'All lean cattle are slaughtered once they're fat enough,' a cynical voice at the back of his mind reminded him.

Bold shook his head. No, that wasn't it. They wouldn't go to all these lengths, even housing him in what seemed close to a palace, just to slaughter him later. Why last night he'd even been sent a beautiful little Burmese girl with his evening rice. She couldn't have been more than fourteen, but had been knowing and willing enough. With explicit gestures, his attendants had indicated that she was his for the night. He had begged off and she had gone away, pouting and mouthing what he assumed were grave doubts about his manhood. So what the devil were his captors up to? He concentrated on what he had seen in the capital during the day. At dawn he had been wakened by the boom of gongs, the clash of cymbals and the blares of long trumpets. Through the window his gaze had fallen on a horde of warriors, clothed in their heathen splendour. There must have been several hundred in that first group, mostly armed with spears and curved swords, but also with flintlocks and muskets. Accompanying them were great elephants, their tusks tipped with gold and with kohl painted around their pink eyes so that they looked like a bunch of monstrous dockside whores. But it was not the elephants' strange decorations which caught Bold's eye. It was the gleaming brass cannon which they carried in the baskets on their backs. The weapons looked as if they might have dated back to the days of Marco Polo – the first to explore this remote and barbaric country – but the gunners who manned the antiquated cannon looked as if they knew how to use them well enough.

Thereafter, hour after hour, there followed similar groups, slogging through the whirling dust, vaunting their hoarse cries and beating their drums as if they wanted the whole world to note their passing. Curious at such large numbers of troops passing northwards, obviously heading for some kind of battle, Bold cursed the fact that he did not speak Burmese. It would be useful intelligence to know who they were and where they were going. Several times he had caught the words 'Maha Bandoola' from the servants as they watched the armed hordes pass by below and he concluded that this must be the name of the local lord in command of these native troops. What was important was that there was going to be a war and it was obvious with whom: the East India Company. And here he was sitting on his thumbs in a golden cage that was a prison. It was very, very vexing.

The following morning John Bold received his first inkling of what was in store for him. Just after breakfast, served in the same smiling, silent fashion that was beginning to grate on his nerves, a small man complete with golden sword thrust through his silken waist-sash, was ushered in. In a very English accent the little Burmese announced, 'My name is Po Hla Gyi. But if you wish you may call me Po, Major Bold.' He pronounced John's name and rank as if they had some significance. Bold's face must have revealed his astonishment at this native addressing him in such perfect English, for he added quickly, 'We are not all ignorant savages, you know, or monkeys straight down from the trees.'

Bold recovered quickly. 'Sorry,' he gasped, 'I didn't

mean to be rude. I was just surprised to hear anyone speaking my own language here – and so well.'

The little Burmese bowed and said, 'Thank you, Major Bold. I have been appointed by our Lord to be your friend and counsellor for the time you spend with us here in Rangoon.'

Bold looked at him sharply. 'You mean that I shall be allowed to leave here some time or another?'

Po smiled at such stupidity. 'Of course, it is obvious, isn't it? I could have had you killed outright on the Island otherwise.'

'*You?*'

'Yes, I was there in the attack, looking for you, you know.'

Now Bold remembered the times between his bouts of unconsciousness when he had imagined that he had heard someone speak English to him. It had not been his delirium. 'But why me?' he asked. Why had the yellow devils risked so many lives just to take him, an obscure major of native cavalry? It made no sense.

Po did not seem to hear his question. Instead he clapped his hands for the servants saying, 'We must go to meet my master, that is why we have brought you all this way.'

Bold felt completely out of his depth.

'I speak of the Lord of the White Elephant and the Golden Foot. Now, Major Bold, we must hurry– a condition which does not come easily to the average Burmese. We are not a hurrying people, but when our master summons us we do.' He smiled and showed his red-stained teeth, at that moment like fangs dripping blood. 'He is not accustomed to waiting for lowly mortals such as we. And he can show his disfavour very dramatically.'

'How?' Bold asked, as one of the half-naked girl servants brought in his boots – now beautifully clean and polished, all traces of the conflict on Shapuree Island vanished. Dutifully she bent her back and allowed him to thrust the tight riding boots on against her skinny body.

33

Po waited till the girl had bowed and disappeared. Very slowly he then drew his long-nailed forefinger across his skinny throat, as if he were slitting it – and enjoying it, too.

5

Off Fort William, Calcutta's docks swarmed with life and movement as preparations for General Cambell's expedition to Rangoon got seriously underway. Small craft plied their trade across the clay-coloured water, they were loaded with stores for the large ships which would carry the troops into battle. Everywhere on the dockside, patrolled by armed sentries to stop pilfering, lay mountains of food and drink for the soldiers: halves of salt pork, mounds of hard biscuits and the precious crates of Bass Pale Ale that would sustain Lord Cavendish's regiment, the white artillerymen and white staff. Next to them lay the piled foodstuffs needed by the sepoys who would make up the bulk of Campbell's force: barrels of cheap wheaten flour for the making of chapattis, great containers of that Indian staple, unhusked rice, plus the many jars of fiery condiments and spices, pickles and the like with which the native troops would flavour their mainly vegetarian diet.

As ever more troops packed the dockside awaiting embarkation, the noise and bustle seemed to increase. From the myriad alleys of the native quarter close by there came the typical smell of India – a rich, heady mixture of curry; ghee; cheap scent; cow dung used as fuel; rotting fruit and urine. From all sides came the wailing noise of native music; the tinkling of bells; the hoarse cries of the hawkers along with the whines of the beggars and the challenges of the shopkeepers squatting cross-legged in their open doorways as they sold their wares. But the thieves in the bright regimentals of Colonel Cavendish's Regiment of Foot neither sensed the smells nor heard the cries of the Indians. Their whole being was fixed exclusively on one sight as they edged by the native quarter and ever closer to the dock. It was the great single carboy of glass, enclosed in a protective basket of wickerwork, now placed to the far end of the jetty – just out of the line of vision of the nearest sepoy sentry who leaned idly on his musket gazing out across the muddy water.

It was a fortnight now since Lord Cavendish had deigned to pay his regiment. A few of them had actually had the audacity to ask the flustered and pot-bellied regimental paymaster why. To be told, 'Well, if you men really want to know, his lordship is waiting for funds from the Horse Guards. Besides he spent a great deal on new regimentals for all of you just before we sailed for Calcutta.' Someone had had the blind temerity to object that the officers were still getting their pay, only to be damned by the Paymaster Lieutenant for insolence. Since then the rank-and-file had undergone a terrible week or so without a visit to the four anna whores of the native quarter, or a pannikin of grog. Even their daily ration of Bass ale had been reduced to one small bottle. And of course the sharp-eyed native money-lenders would not do business with them, however much they protested they would pay the debt back as soon as they received their next pay. The wise baboos, used to the wiles of the British soldiery, reasoned that most of them would be dead by the time they got their next pay. If the Burmese didn't finish them off, the fever would.

Now the bunch of desperate men crept closer to the lovely glowing carboy, set so temptingly on the section of empty quay. For the glass bottle promised glorious oblivion – at least until their trooper sailed. For it contained 'Nelson's Blood', prime naval grog which had not been watered down like that handed out to the Army. 'Make yer frigging hair curl,' one of the little party had ventured, licking parched lips in anticipation. 'Put lead in yer pencil and hair on yer chest,' another commented, and added with a malicious sneer, 'and put a few frigging wrinkles in frigging Lord Cavendish's frigging precious regimentals, too, I'll be bound, mates!'

'Ay, lads,' the others had agreed *sotto voce*, already

savouring the monumental booze-up to come. For there were at least five gallons of dark Navy rum in the carboy. But the would-be thieves were fated not to enjoy that fiery dark-brown tipple.

Just as they cleared the last of the stinking native hovels, five yards away, a well-remembered voice bellowed in the tones of his native Northumberland, 'Standfast, you damned rogues! Standfast, will yer?' Next moment 'Geordie Jem' sprang in front of them, the pike which was the sign of his office held at the ready, with a half dozen men behind him, bayonets already fixed and levelled.

The thieves stopped in their tracks, faces suddenly blanched. 'Holy Mother o' God, Jesus and Mary,' Private O'Sullivan quavered, and crossed himself hastily, 'Tis the frigging Provost Sergeant hissen!'

'And well may you cross yourself, you thieving villain,' Lord Cavendish hissed. 'You shall pay hard for having brought disgrace to *my* regiment!'

'A trap,' O'Sullivan moaned, as the men of the provost section started to advance on them, bayonets levelled, '*A bluidy English trap!*'

One hour later Lord Cavendish's battalion was drawn up in a three-sided square, the open end facing the dock. In the centre of the square the provost squad had erected a make-shift flogging triangle, in front of which the miscreants, heads hanging, shirts already ripped from their backs, lined up to await their punishment. All were bitter with the knowledge that they had walked straight into their fate. Lord Cavendish had deliberately planted that carboy of rum there to tempt fools like them into attempting to steal it. He now faced his regiment, peering through his eyeglass though his vision was as good as the next man's. 'I *will* have discipline in my regiment!' he commenced. 'On board ship coming out here you have become slack and rebellious. That must cease forthwith! Soon I shall have the honour of leading my regiment into battle. But I do not intend to take a rabble of ill-disciplined thieves into that battle with me. I want soldiers, disciplined soldiers, who will obey the legitimate orders of their officers without question.'

'Get that frigger in front o' me,' O'Sullivan whispered out of the side of his mouth, 'and I'll be putting a frigging ball right into his frigging back. I swear it on my mother's blood – I frigging well will!' But the Irishman fell silent as the Provost Sergeant Geordie Jem glared at him, as he toyed with the 'cat'. He didn't want any 'special' treatment.

Lord Cavendish stepped back and cried in a weak voice which always failed to carry to the end of the parade, 'Adjutant, take over!'

Lieutenant Sweeney, the Adjutant, was a veteran of the Peninsula Wars and Waterloo who still remained a lieutenant at the age of fifty because he had neither the money nor patronage to be able to climb the ladder of promotion. As he stepped out into the glare of the centre of the square, his face was set in a look of distaste. He didn't like Cavendish, he didn't like the trap he had set for his own men and he didn't like flogging. He felt it only brutalized the men even further. But he *did* need this last commission in India. There was the prospect of loot in the coming campaign in Burma and he desperately needed hard cash for the years of retirement to come. So he did what was expected of him. 'Regimental Surgeon!' he bellowed in a voice that carried to the furthest rank of the square. Cawing in hoarse protest at being startled in this way, the vultures rose lazily into the merciless Indian sky.

As the little doctor hurried forward, with his satchel slung over his shoulder, followed by his attendants with their jugs of water and vinegar, he turned to the brawny men of the provost squad. 'String the first prisoner up!' he commanded. As they proceeded with their task, Geordie Jem grinned and raising the cat-o'-nine-tails, letting it drop heavily into his calloused palm. The whip was a deceptively flimsy looking instrument – it weighed a mere three pounds. But each of its nine lashes was knotted nine times and each knot contained a tiny piece of lead. When

Geordie Jem let loose with it, eighty-one pieces of jagged lead slashed against the victim's back, ripping the naked flesh away like so many tiny razors. In the hands of an expert like the Provost Sergeant the 'cat' could lay a man's back bare to the naked bones by the time fifty lashes, the minimum, had been laid on.

'Provost Sergeant,' the Adjutant cried as the first man was strapped to the triangle, his pale white back already glistening with sweat. Whereupon Geordie Jem stepped forward and flexed his bulging muscles, an unholy grin on his face. The drummer, who would be used to count the strokes, tensed. The prisoner on the triangle hunched. He knew what was coming. He prepared his body for the shock, tensing his every muscle. The Provost Sergeant raised the whip. The lashes flared out. With a grunt he aimed a savage blow at the prisoner's back, just above the kidneys where the lashes tore into the flesh. Instantly blood welled up in bright red pears along the length of the blow.

'*One!*' the drummer cried, and beat his drum. Lord Cavendish nodded in approval. Now let the NCO lay on all his might. By the time he had reached a count of ten, the thieving swine would be screaming out in pain for him to stop and there were another forty lashes to go after that.

Red-faced and sweating already, Geordie Jem began to lay into the prisoner, taking great care and sadistic pleasure in criss-crossing the man's whole back. 'When I've done 'em,' he was wont to boast to his cronies over a pannikin of grog in the mess after a flogging, 'there's nary a piece of solid flesh left on their bleeding backs. Geordie Jem,' and here he usually poked a sausage-like thumb at his brawny chest in pride, 'leaves his mark on 'em for the rest of their frigging lives!'

Now he prepared to do just that. But on this January afternoon fate had other plans. For just as the pale-face drummer, nauseated by the sight of the blood now streaming down the moaning prisoner's back, had cried out thickly, '*Twenty-five!*', there was a furious clatter of hooves. Forgetting the iron discipline of the British Army in their surprise, hundreds of heads turned to the open end of the great square where they saw an amazing sight. A general in full highland rig, including bushy black bonnet, riding hell-for-leather along the quay, his kilts flying up and yelling his head off.

'The blessed saints preserve us,' O'Sullivan cried in awe, 'it's the bluidy Hieland Laddie hissen!'

Lord Cavendish visibly blanched as he saw General Campbell bearing down on him in full gallop, followed by his staff, who were doing their utmost to keep up with the irate commander. He wasn't the only one affected. Geordie Jem was so taken aback by the spectacle that he faltered in mid-stroke, while the drummer actually dropped a drumstick to the dust. In an instant all was confusion as a sweating General Campbell, tugging furiously at the reins of his lathered mount so that it reared up into the air forelegs flailing, cried in anger, 'Will you stop this flogging, sir . . . !

'Stop it, sir?' Cavendish echoed foolishly, as Campbell glared down at him from the back of his big grey. 'But these men attempted to commit a crime, sir,' he stuttered.

'Then they must be punished. But I shall tell you this my Lord Cavendish, in the Company's Army we do not flog – not even our black sepoys, do you hear, sir?'

Lord Cavendish's face flushed with shame as he realised that the old Scot was making an absolute fool of him in front of his own regiment, one that had cost his doting father thousands upon thousands of pounds. 'But sir,' he protested, 'we do not belong to the East India Company Army. We are in the King's service.'

Campbell glared down at him. 'Are you an absolute imbecile, mon,' he declared, 'or d'ye have trouble understanding the English o' yer forebairns?' In his anger General Campbell was reverting to the language of his own 'forebairns'. 'Have ye nae taken the trouble to read the KR's?' – he meant the King's Regulations. When Lord Cavendish shook his head, at a loss for words, Campbell elucidated. 'Then I'll tell yer what they say, Colonel.

When an English regiment serves in the subcontinent it must obey the rules and practices of the East India Company. Its allegiance is transferred to the Governor-General – and that means – *no flogging*! He spat the words out venomously. 'Now no more of ye blather. Have yon poor fellow cut down,' he indicated the man hanging limply at the triangle, 'and see that you punish the rest in some other way.'

O'Sullivan, the irrepressible Irishman, raised his right hand and cried into the sudden stillness, 'Three cheers, lads, for his Honour. Hip . . . hip . . . '

The first hurrah rang out from half a thousand throats. But Campbell would have nothing of it. He raised himself in his stirrups and cried, 'Huish, lads . . . huish!' The cheering died away raggedly and the General sat down in his saddle again, the rage gone from his face to be replaced by a look of almost sadness. 'Don't cheer me, lads,' he said when silence was restored. 'For you have nothing to cheer me for. It won't be long now afore I'll be leading ye on a hazardous undertaking. We shall be victorious over the yellow heathen beyond yon sea, I'm confident o' that. But ye can be sure that some of us won't be coming back.' He shook his greying head 'that is the way of war. That is why we all took the King's shulling in the first place.' He sat there heavily on his horse, as if he did not know what to do next.

The Adjutant thought for him, his eyes full of admiration for a real soldier. 'General Officer on parade,' he cried in that tremendous parade-ground voice of his. 'Present – PRESENT ARMS!' As the battalion's bayonets flashed and the red-coated infantry came to the salute, hands slapping the sides of their muskets, the Adjutant threw the General a tremendous salute.

Campbell returned the courtesy and then said quietly, 'Dismiss the parade, Adjutant . . . Colonel Cavendish, could I have a minute of your time please?' Campbell leaned down from his saddle, then he selected his words carefully; he had need of Lord Cavendish and his Foot. 'In due course, Colonel,' he said as the soldiers hurried to find whatever shade there was on the docks, chattering busily among themselves about the sudden turn of events, 'we shall be facing the enemy at Rangoon. As you have already said, we know nothing of their dispositions there. There could be severe fighting as a result and as you well know, Colonel, it has always been reckoned that an attacker needs three times the number of the defender to succeed. I am sure now that we will not possess that ratio at Rangoon.'

'Agreed, sir. but I have always believed that any white man is worth ten natives,' Cavendish answered pompously.

Campbell sighed like a weary schoolmaster with a very slow pupil. 'Possibly. At all events, Colonel, my white artillerymen and your regiment of foot are going to form the basis of my attack. Everything will depend upon the steadfastness of your men.'

'You can count on me – and them, sir,' Cavendish said stoutly, though he felt a sudden icy finger of fear trace its way down the small of his back, as he realised that soon fellow human beings would be shooting at him – *and aiming to kill*! Why the devil had his father – the silly old fool – contrived to buy him the regiment in the first place?

'I am relying on it,' Campbell said, though there was a note of doubt in his voice. 'But to ensure that you have the best possible chances in the assault, Colonel, I am going to attach another formation to your regiment. A squadron of native cavalry who will proceed your assault and obtain all possible intelligence on the enemy's dispositions before you blunder into them unwittingly.'

Cavendish's face set in a sudden sneer. '*Black niggahs!*' he exclaimed. 'Oh, I say, what next?'

Campbell shook his head. 'Yes,' he said, 'black niggahs who have fought – *and died* – for the Company for nair on ten years now.' His voice rose as the sudden clatter of many hooves drowned even the noises coming from the native quarter. 'And here they come, Colonel Cavendish – *Bold's Horse!*' Silently he wished to God at that moment that their commander were still alive to lead them. . . .

6

The palace chamber was of barbaric splendour. From the walls of the great throne room hung canopies of Nanking velvet. The mosaic floor was worked in strange intricate, sometimes obscene, designs. Gold and ivory decorations were everywhere. Indeed the very throne upon which rested the Lord of the White Elephant and the Golden Foot consisted solely of carved ivory embellished with a multitude of jewels and precious stones. All was opulence and a kind of overdone Oriental splendour which John Bold found slightly nauseating. This was the second day that he had attended the court in order to be introduced to the Lord of the White Elephant – so far without success. Now he squatted on a silken cushion next to Po, listlessly watching the efforts of the teenage dancing girls. They were pretty, he had to admit, and completely naked beneath the transparent yellow robes – he could see that Burmese women shaved their pubic hair off as did the Indians – but they moved too slowly to excite him and all the while the musicians – if one could call them that – kept banging golden gongs.

If Bold were bored by the slow, jerky movements of the sweating dancers, Po was intrigued. He craned his head forward, dark eyes greedily drinking in the movements of the lithe girlish bodies and their tiny, rose-tipped breasts. Bold only grinned slightly and out of the corner of his eye studied the Lord of the White Elephant. His ancient parchment-like face showed no animation. His thin claws of hands, their long nails sheathed in gold, remained listlessly in the lap of his rich silken robe. Despite his power and the richness of his apparel, Bold saw that he was really a frail old man, wasted by age and illness. He was not one bit interested in the intricate gyrations of the dancing girls who had been summoned for John Bold's entertainment. But why should this all-powerful ruler, who could have had him murdered already, wish to entertain him? Of what use was a captured major of native cavalry to him?

That morning as they had again proceeded from his luxurious prison to the palace, he had posed that same question once more to Po. They had been passing the fabled Golden Pagoda, its beautiful steps defiled and stained with betel juice, the urine of half-naked children who seemed to squat there all the time and the faeces of wandering pi-dogs. Po had given his usual bland smile and not answered. Instead he had asked a somewhat surprising question of his own. Pointing to the temple he'd queried: 'What do you think of the Pagoda as a defensive position, Major Bold?'

John Bold was caught completely off balance by the question and protested, ' . . . but it's a sort of church.'

'But you are not a follower of Buddha,' Po had persisted, 'so please answer.'

'Well,' Bold had ventured. 'It is the highest point in the city, as far as I can see. From up there any defender could dominate the whole of Rangoon.'

'Exactly. I should imagine that your excellent General Campbell in Calcutta would give his precious kilt to possess that information, eh.' And with that remark, the significance of which John Bold realized only long afterwards, Po fell silent and would not be drawn any further. But now as the beating of the gongs ceased and the dancing girls came to the end of their display, Bold's curiosity was at last to be satisfied. For as they ran out of the throne room, their bottoms jiggling nicely through the transparent robes, the Lord of the White Elephant beckoned with his claw-like hand and croaked one word, 'Bold.'

Po sprang to his feet immediately. 'Quick, he calls!' he hissed and bending so low that Bold felt his turban head-dress might fall off at any moment, he approached the throne. There, with Bold standing next to him, he awaited the old man's command.

The ruler let him wait while he studied Bold. Bold did the same and concluded that the Lord of the White Elephant was a man who in all his long life had never been denied anything. At last he spoke, while all around the courtiers remained absolutely silent. Po listened attentively, as if his very life depended upon it, and then translated: 'It is our intention, my lord says, that our armies will march into India and take back those territories east of Moorshedabad, which belonged to the Kingdom of Arracan – conquered by my lord's father in the Christian year of 1783 and later stolen by the English.'

Bold nodded as if confirming the old man's statement. Next moment he felt himself a complete fool. The Lord of the White Elephant and the Golden Foot had never needed anyone's approval or acknowledgement throughout his whole long life.

The ruler spoke again and once more Po translated: 'Now we understand that your Governor General Amherst will have the temerity to oppose us. He will try to stop our drive on Calcutta. This we have anticipated. But we do not fear him or his soldiers. Those Indian coolies are rabble. They will run in panic from the first Burmese warrior they see. However, we have a problem. It is many years since any of my people have ventured further than the Arracan. India beyond there is unknown to us. We know nothing of the fortifications, the earthworks and the like which your Company has built closer to Calcutta in these last fifty years or so. We need someone who does.' The ruler fixed Bold with his unblinking gaze and at once the Englishman realised why he had been spared. 'Someone like you, Major Bold.'

Bold looked desperately from the ruler to Po, who told him, 'The lord says if you accept you will be granted the Golden Umbrella, a high honour in our country.'

Bold did not know what the 'Golden Umbrella' was or give a damn about it; he was too shocked. 'But that would mean betrayal of my own people!' he blurted out. Yet at the same time a voice at the back of his mind asked himself, 'What people? Your mother was French, your

45

father an Irishman. And what reward did you get for being a loyal subject of His Majesty? Why you were chased out of Europe – and your native country – for ever!' Bold ignored the voice and turned his head a little to get the best of the cooler air wafted in their direction by the punkah wallah. For a few moments there was a heavy silence and his mind raced. They had spared his life for their own purpose and they could take it just as well if he did not fulfil that purpose. In the meantime they could attempt to break him down, bend him to their will. He knew the tricks of the Orient by now. They would use the old 'sweet and sour' technique. First would come the 'sweet' – drugs, bribes, women, promises. Inspite of what occidentals said, the oriental mind was not all that subtle. They felt every man had his price. But when the 'sweet' didn't work, they would resort to the 'sour'. There would be blows, then threats of what would follow and finally there'd be torture. In the end – death.

John Bold made a quick decision. He knew that he would not succumb to the 'sour' treatment if it came. He had not much interest in living, because there was no person in the whole wide world to whom he was special. But he did not want to lose his honour by betraying the country which had betrayed him so badly. Still he was not prepared to suffer torture unnecessarily, so he must prevaricate until he found a way out. He risked a weak smile at the Lord of the White Elephant, trying to appear undecided, yet compliant. 'Po,' he said slowly, as if finding it difficult to choose the right words, 'tell your lord that I am an honourable man . . . I cannot betray my old comrades just like that . . . I need time to think about it.'

Hurriedly Po translated his words. The ruler nodded and then slowly unbent his right hand, blemished by scores of liver spots, to hold up three gold-tipped claws. Even before Po interpreted, Bold knew what he had said. He had three days to consider.

When the ruler looked away, as if Bold no longer existed, Po bowed low and proceeded to back away from the presence, taking Bold with him. Moments later they were outside in the ante-chamber, and while Bold's mind raced at the new prospect facing him Po declared, 'You should thank your god that is over. The Lord of the White Elephant is very touchy. One wrong word and . . . ' he didn't finish the sentence, as if he feared putting his thoughts into words. 'Why, once he had a courtier who displeased him impaled on a golden rod. They placed the rod in his anus and then men with hammers . . . ' Again he let the sentence trail away unfinished, shuddering violently, as if he had just been struck by a chill wind. The Burmese was petrified with fear.

Once outside Po's confidence returned. He pointed to the waiting tonga, its curtains drawn against the morning heat. 'It is for you, Major Bold. A present from my lord, please go and examine his genorosity.'

Frowning a little, Bold walked over to the carriage and drew back the curtain. A woman sat there motionless, her dark eyes staring into nothing, but there was no denying her beauty and that of her breasts, nudging through the delicate material of her blouse. Bold noted, too, that the little finger of her right hand was gilded: something which indicated virginity in Burma. The 'sweet' was already beginning. They were offering him a virgin!

'She is a princess,' Po said cheerfully, as the Burmese beauty stared ahead, her face demure and set, but with a kind of sadness in her dark eyes. 'A minor one admittedly, but she is yours while you stay in Rangoon to use as you wish!' Chuckling, he formed a ring with his right hand and thrust his left forefinger through it vigorously, making his meaning all too clear.

The princess, her mien always sad and serious, followed Bold everywhere within the golden cage that was his prison, even to his bedroom on the first night. It was obvious she was prepared to do her duty, but John had the impression she was not going to do it gladly. That first night he had gently shooed her from his bedside and had earned a faint smile for his efforts, as though she was glad that this white man, whose language she could not speak, did not want to take her virginity.

John Bold was glad for a different reason. He had three days to escape. His time was limited and nights would be the only time when he could scout around unobserved – the servants would be asleep or high on bhang. As for sentries, he had so far not been able to ascertain whether there were any guarding his golden cage. His plan was rudimentary. Some two hundred yards away he had spotted a large wood of palms and the like. That would be his first objective. From there he would head for the estuary below Rangoon where he would steal or buy a boat. Already he had secreted one of the golden plates on which his food was served and hoped he might use that as barter. He knew that he would have to flee by boat, for he had already realized he would not survive long in a country whose language he did not speak and where he would be instantly recognized as a foreigner. He knew, too, that the biggest problem would only commence once he had managed to obtain such a boat – the crossing of the Bay of Bengal without a chart and with only the sun and the stars by which to navigate. But there really was no other alternative. So he set his mind to taking it all step by step, rigidly solving one problem at a time before tackling the next, and the first was to ascertain if there *were* any sentries or where they were located. His bedroom was situated at the top of the golden cage, some three floors up. Below him were the living rooms and the room in which he ate. Below that he guessed were the servant quarters and at the moment he had no desire to make them suspicious by wandering around in the middle of the night.

That first night he stared for hours at the garden three stories below, straining his eyes to penetrate the glowing tropical darkness in an attempt to spot any movement. He reasoned that any sentries outside would have to be changed at periodic intervals. But by one o'clock that morning, with a sickle moon spreading its light down below, he gave up. There had been absolutely nothing. The whole house lay in silence, not even a single dog barked. It was as if he were all alone in the whole wide world. For a long while he slumped there at the window. It was just before dawn that he came up with the answer as to the identity of his guard. Po had been his watchdog at first. Now he had gone, and it was the princess who had replaced him. She had been with him all day long. Po and his master had obviously reasoned she would be with him all night, too. Even now, he told himself, she might well be awake in the next bedroom, listening intently for the slightest movement he might make. Bold bit his lip. To begin his escape, which would be via the bottom floor, he dare not risk trying to descend by the outer wall as he would have to pass by her bedroom. She might well give the alarm in an instant and he would be discovered. The sun had already slid over the horizon to the east and from below there were the first stirrings of the servants, when Bold finally found the solution. He slapped his clenched right fist into the palm of his other hand with the joy of his realization, but what he planned to do wasn't pleasant. . . .

TWO: ESCAPE FROM THE GOLDEN PAGODA

1

General Campbell had long overcome the problem of sea-sickness which now afflicted so many of his expeditionary force. Sometimes it seemed to the craggy-faced Scot he had spent half his life on troopers such as this – the men going down with sickness and cholera. Or being driven half-mad by the baking heat of the dark holds in which they were confined, so that officers had to be posted with loaded pistols on the decks above while the sailors swamped the soldiers below with bucket after bucket of seawater in an attempt to cool them off. But on this third day of the voyage out across the Bay of Bengal, the heat ripples rising off the water like a grey fog back in his native 'Auld Reekie', he was afflicted by a feeling of uncertainty.

The British Army was the world's largest and most professional and since the turn of the century it had enjoyed victory after victory. They'd experienced a few bad knocks, of course, during the Peninsula War in Spain, but Old Boney had been defeated in the end. Ever since then in the many wars the John Company had fought in India against the princes, there had never been a real defeat. The Horse Guards, Parliament and Calcutta had grown accustomed to success and the powers-that-be would not tolerate anything else. Yet, all Campbell's long experience told him that this expedition to Rangoon, based on the Governor-General's own plan, was a very risky undertaking and if it failed, Archie Campbell would take the blame, not my Lord Amherst. Naturally he did not subscribe to the belief that the Burmese were ferocious unstoppable warriors which was current in some circles in Calcutta. From what little he knew of the country and its people he had nothing but contempt for them. They ate revolting things like monkey's brain scouped from the still living animal and sickening fare such as unborn mice

53

and snakes cooked alive in boiling rice. People like that couldn't possibly make good soldiers. But undoubtedly there would be *thousands* of the heathen devils and he had only one white regiment of foot under command. Of course he trusted his sepoys, but he was too much of a realist not to know they could be rattled easily. Everything, at least during the assault, depended upon the steadfastness of his British infantry, and his particular regiment of British infantry was commanded by a man without experience who was an arrogant fool to boot! But he would have to make do with what he had. Cavendish's men were good enough, of course: the usual mix of old sweats and new recruits, culled from the slums of England and the starving villages of Ireland. As long as their officers allowed them to get drunk periodically, gamble at cards and visit the 'angel house', they would follow them happily to the ends of the earth for three shillings and sixpence a week. But although they had fewer rights than some convict serving a sentence of hard labour in Dartmoor, Campbell knew they took offence easily. If their officers started to treat them like animals, they rebelled. To Campell's way of thinking, Lord Cavendish *was* treating his men badly. Why couldn't he allow them to come topside for an hour or two each day, for example? Why was he so miserably mean in allowing them no more than one bottle of Bass Light Ale between two men per day? In this climate a white man needed to drink gallons of liquid daily in order to make up for sweat loss. The way the rank-and-file saw it, they were being treated like coolies – and they wouldn't stand that for ever. 'Damn the man!' he cursed silently to himself and stared hard at the fop, who had not one ounce of sense in his whole body. Of course, he could order Cavendish to improve the treatment of his men, but that would only cause bad blood. Cavendish had powerful friends at court and after all his uncle was the Governor-General! But still he had to do something which would ensure the success of the initial assault force, Cavendish's foot. Clearing his throat noisely he strode, kilt swinging, to the other side of the quarter deck where Captain Hamilton, a fellow Scot and another veteran of the long war against Napoleon, conned the ship.

Hamilton, a no-nonsense fellow like most of Lord Nelson's former captains, rapped out an order to a junior officer and barked, 'Well General, where's the trouble?'

Despite his mood, Campbell's craggy face cracked into a smile. Hamilton didn't believe in beating about the bush. 'It's that damned Colonel Cavendish,' he snorted, 'he's treating his men abominably.'

'Rum, buggery and the lash, that's all those creatures know,' Hamilton rasped.

'Well,' Campbell said, watching the barefoot swabs throwing fresh buckets of seawater down the hold, 'all that concerns me, Hamilton, is to have yon fellahs fighting fit when we get to Rangoon. Let me ask you a question.'

'Fire away, General.'

'When do you expect landfall in the Andaman Isles?'

Hamilton looked up at the dazzling blue sky, as if some celestial map were traced upon it and answered, 'If we can keep up this speed, General, two more days.'

Campbell nodded, 'Then we can keep them from going mad or mutinying till then. I'm going to order a bottle of Bass per man this day out of my own personal stock. That should help.'

'Uncommonly generous of you, General,' Hamilton commented, tongue-in-cheek. 'You did say you were a Scot, didn't you?'

Campbell gave a soft chuckle. 'Dinna fear, Captain, I'll charge it to the Governor-General in due course. It'll be a small price to pay for extending the British Empire. Now,' Campbell was very serious again, 'I am tempted to let Cavendish's foot have two days rest in the islands. Give them a chance to swim and eat fresh cooked food instead of cold sowbelly and hardtack. In the meantime I'd like to send off my cavalry – those native irregulars Bold's Horse, ye ken – to land on the Irrawaddy and gather what intelligence they can before I send in my assault.' Campbell pointed to the steam vessel *HMS Diana* bravely ploughing through the sea half a mile away and trailing a cloud of thick black smoke behind her from her tall funnel. 'Now what think ye the time it'd take for yon steam kettle, with sails, to reach the Irrawaddy from the islands, laden with a half a squadron o' horse?'

Again Captain Hamilton looked at the sky and said after a moment or two's consideration, 'With a favourable wind – five days. But her lascars would have to work mighty canny to keep her boilers supplied with coal to do it.'

'Lascars'll do anything for money,' Campbell dismissed that little problem easily. 'So let us hope that Cavendish's poor swine can be kept under control until we reach the islands.'

'There's always rum and the lash, as employed by His Majesty's Royal Navy,' Hamilton suggested.

Campbell shook his grizzled head. 'There'll be no lash in my command,' he said firmly, 'and as I've got no rum for them, they'll have to make do with the Governor-General's free bottle of ale. Pray God that it will keep them sweet for another day.'

'It only confirms my own assessment of the Scot,' Lord Cavendish said to the Adjutant, Lieutenant Sweeney, as the two of them stood on the scrubbed white deck, watching the lowering of the crates of beer to the hold below. 'He is one step above your dirty Irishman, who has, as everyone knows, absolutely no wit at all. He is cleaner, your Scot, but still he is a half-wit. Campbell proves the rule.' He sniffed slightly, as if he had just caught a whiff of the unpleasant stench coming from below – a mixture of faeces, human sweat and despair. 'Fie, imagine giving that rabble a whole bottle of beer each; the man's molly-coddling the idle rogues!'

Sweeney ventured cautiously, 'The bosun says the temperature down there is well over a hundred, sir.'

'Yes, and it'll help them to sweat some of the fat off their useless bodies,' Cavendish answered. 'My God, why couldn't Papa have bought me a cavalry regiment instead

56

of that mob. At least the cavalry don't serve in these remote God-forsaken climes.'

'Yessir,' Sweeney said dutifully, knowing that there was no reasoning with the man. Undoubtedly he had been brought up on some great estate where the servants had been treated like cattle and human beings commenced at the rank of baronet. Cavendish had absolutely no feeling for the common man. Sweeney raised his hand to his shako, 'Permission to be excused sir?' he requested. 'I shall go over to see that the men behave themselves while the General is present.'

'As you wish, Adjutant,' Cavendish sighed, 'if you think it is important.' He patted his forehead delicately with a lace handkerchief plucked from his sleeve. Sweeney's nostrils were suddenly assailed by the smell of expensive cologne. 'I think I shall get out of this intolerable heat – I do declare I'm getting in quite a lather, just like a country bumpkin. I think I shall have a lie-down in my cabin. I do hope that fool of a servant of mine has thought to cool the champers.' And with that he was gone, leaving Sweeney to stare at his back, his face a mixture of contempt and frustrated rage.

'A penny for 'em, Lieutenant . . . er. . . . '

The Adjutant swung round and stiffened to attention, 'Sweeney, sir,' he snapped, saluting smartly.

Campbell waved for him to desist. 'Far too hot for that kind of thing, Sweeney,' he said, eyeing the other man's scarred, brick-red face and liking what he saw. Here was a soldier, he told himself: a hard man but a fair one. He'd know how to lead – and how to look after – good men. His mind made up, General Campbell took the plunge. He told the slightly bemused Lieutenant, who was not used to the confidences of a general officer, his plans: how he intended to rest the Cavendish Battalion in the Andaman Islands and how he intended to send Bold's Horse ahead in the *Diana*. 'But after all they are cavalry, Sweeney,' he added. 'Their job is to cover ground, not to take and hold it. The latter is the task of infantry, don't you agree?'

'Why yes sir, of course,' Sweeney replied automatically, wondering where all this was leading.

'Now Sweeney, since I first talked this over with yon Captain Hamilton, I've had further thoughts on the matter. I need infantry ashore too, while the cavalry are searching for intelligence. I need a force to form a bridgehead prior to starting the assault. You see, once the Burmese are aware of our presence on the Irrawaddy, they will surely attack. Therefore I have to have a firm base on land before they do so.'

Sweeney nodded, suddenly thinking hard. The lack of a firm bridgehead on land before the main force had come ashore had been the cause of the British Army's defeats at Dunkirk and Walcheren back at the turn of the century. Christ, in that same damned flat stretch of Dutch countryside he had been wounded twice in the first week of the attack and had been forced to run for his life with Old Boney's heavy dragoons hot on his heels. He risked a question. 'Would you need men from Colonel Lord Cavendish's battalion, sir?'

'Exactly, Sweeney. I'd like to see a company at least go ashore with the Horse and dig in on the beach to cover the subsequent landings – once the Horse have ascertained where exactly the enemy positions are.'

'The battalion would be honoured, sir,' Sweeney said dutifully.

Campbell looked at him quizzically. 'Do you really mean that, Sweeney? I can't see my Lord Cavendish wanting to split up his precious battalion in that way, can you?' Campbell said. 'It was purchased for him by his father and he regards it not as part of the British Army, but as his own personal property to do with as he wishes.' He shook his head. 'I know the system's wrong and one day it will be changed. but as things stand we must work within it.' He paused to let the words sink in.

Down in the hold they were singing now. The alcohol had gone to their heads. But the effect of the free beer wouldn't last long, Sweeney knew. They would have sweated it out of their emaciated bodies within the hour. Soon they would be crying out for more water, fresh air, new latrine buckets – anything to get them out of that stifling hold for a few moments – the poor swine.

Campbell lowered his voice. 'Lieutenant Sweeney, you are an old soldier as I am. You know the penalty for disobeying orders. Now I am certain that Colonel Cavendish will *not* relinquish that company of foot I need to make the landings a success.' The Scot looked carefully from left to right, fearful that he might be overheard. 'But what if your Colonel – hm – lost a company before he knew it?'

'But how would he do that, sir?' Sweeney stuttered, totally bewildered.

'*I-diddle-diddle . . . I've got her on my fiddle . . . roll me over an' do it agen . . .*' they were singing drunkenly in the hold now. Despite his mood, General Campbell smiled. Typical British footsloggers and irrepressible, he told himself.

'What, Sweeney,' he continued, selecting his words carefully, 'if during that couple of days' rest in the islands – say at night – one of your Colonel's companies was spirited aboard the *Diana*? The sentries would be alerted in advance naturally and there would be the least possible noise.' He gazed hard at the Adjutant from beneath his beetling grey eyebrows. 'It wouldn't be too difficult.'

'You are thinking of me, sir?' Sweeney said warily.

Campbell nodded. 'And if the mission is carried out successfully, you have my word of honour that there'll be a captaincy waiting for you in the John Company when we arrive back in India – and no questions asked.' He chuckled, seeing that Sweeney was already beginning to weaken. The poor fellow had probably been a simple Lieutenant for thirty years or more. 'Besides remember, Sweeney, first come, first served. Those who get into Rangoon first will have the choice of the loot. That's the way it has always been in the British Army.'

Down in the hold, as Sweeney gathered his thoughts, they were bawling, '*Now this is number four . . . and I've got her on the floor . . . roll me over an' do it agen . . . roll me in the clover. . . . '*

'I don't think I'd have much trouble in getting the first company to follow me,' he said sucking his teeth, 'all the officers are like myself, sir, old sweats at the end of their careers with not much to hope for. But let me ask you a question, if I may be so bold, sir. What happens if I fail?'

Campbell chuckled, but there was little warmth in the laugh. 'Then, there's only one thing for it, isn't there? The only advice I can give you on that score is to come back a handsome corpse.'

'All or nothing, then, sir?'

'Now this is number seven – and she ain't half in heaven . . . roll me over an' do it again. . . . '

But now the two soldiers facing each other on deck no longer heard the drunken singing from the hold or the snap and crack of the taut sails above their heads. Each was wrapped up in a cocoon of thoughts and forebodings. Suddenly Sweeney brightened. 'Sir,' he whispered with fervour, 'what other chance will an officer of my age be given? I'll do it!'

The die had been cast. At that moment, with the drunken infantry singing their ribald ditty in the depths of the stinking hold, two soldiers had ensured the success of Britain's first war against Burma, and unwittingly helped to save John Bold's life.

'Now this is number ten and she's at it once agen . . . roll me over in the clover and do it agen . . . roll me. . . . '

2

In Rangoon it had been a long hot day. The golden cage had sweltered in the overwhelming heat and the princess, usually so silent, had demanded ice-cold drinks all afternoon.

John Bold had made a pretence of being absolutely bored. For her benefit and that of the servants, he had yawned a great deal and lounged on the silken divans, picking in an idle manner at his food. In reality, however, his mind was racing electrically as he waited for the night. Indeed he had to restrain himself almost physically from getting up and doing the things he knew had to be done before nightfall. For on the morrow he was supposed to announce his decision to the Lord of the White Elephant and the Golden Foot, and it was going to be a decision that the Burmese ruler could not accept. So tonight must see his escape!

He had not been as idle as it appeared. Surreptitiously he had palmed one of the little fruit knives the servants had laid for dealing with the after-dinner pomelos and mangoes. The blade was blunt, but it did have a sharp point on it. It now rested down his boot and he counted it alongside the gold plate he had already stolen to buy the boat he would need. Further to that a portion of his midday rice, spiced with an evil-smelling fish paste and curry, had been covertly wrapped in a napkin and placed hurriedly beneath the divan while the princess had been looking the other way. With it had vanished three cinnamon-spiced rice buns. Together, they should be sufficient to keep him for a day or two, and water he would have to scoop from the paddies or buffalo-wallows.

Now he waited with increasing impatience as the dying sun sank beneath the distant hills and the interior of the golden cage gradually became cooler. From where he lay on the divan, pretending ennui, he could see the swaying bamboos and sensed the quickening pulse of the night to come: it was there in the click and buzz of a million insects; the hoarse croak of the bullfrogs in the paddyfields and the soft grunt of unknown animals as they ventured out for water.

Soon he, too, would be venturing out into the unknown, with every man's hand against him. Now everything depended upon the princess sitting cross-legged opposite him. What lay behind that beautiful oval mask he wondered? In his decade in India, John Bold had taken many of the native women. It was the custom; all white men did if they did not want to go crazy from loneliness and frustration. There simply weren't enough British women to go round. He knew how willing the local females were; they had been taught with their mother's milk that their purpose in life was to please their man and bear him children, preferably male ones. Unlike the simpering white girls of 'the fishing fleet', they had been surrounded by raw, naked sex all their lives: from the exotic dancing whores of Lord Krishna painted in the friezes to the myriad complicated sexual positions of the Kamasutra and the licentious nymphs of Hindu mythology. Sex was part and parcel of their daily existence.

Now as he stared at the princess through lowered eyelashes, he wondered if she would be the same, although she was a virgin and apparently high-born. She looked much like the other women he had enjoyed. Her breasts were high, firm and circular unlike those of English women. She had the same tiny waist accentuated by plump hips and belly which Oriental men liked. Undoubtedly her loins would be shaven and deeply cleft, the naked skin dusted with saffron. Would she surrender to him without protest? John Bold was hardened by the tricks fate had played upon him since he was a boy and had become brutalized by nearly ten years of campaigning against the savage tribes of Northern India, yet this night he hesitated to do what he had to. He felt an ever increasing reluctance to use the beautiful girl opposite him.

Outside the last gong had boomed half an hour ago. Soon, Bold knew, all of Rangoon would be asleep until the first light of dawn woke them once more. Here in a capital where there were no theatres, music halls, band concerts and the like, the inhabitants slept when their chickens did and rose with the rooster. It was time to be moving.

He levered himself from the divan purposefully. He felt her looking at him in the glowing darkness. Poor girl, if she were really the watchdog he suspected, then the dog had to be put to sleep. 'You will come with me now,' he commanded, feeling a growing sense of excitement. 'Come, please.'

Although she had not understood the words, she had comprehended their sense. Obediently she trailed after him. 'Get into bed,' he ordered and pointed. Dutifully she went across to it and began taking off her clothes. He did the same, carefully placing the clothes near the door and when she turned, he stole outside to retrieve his food parcel and slip it hurriedly among them.

Now she lay on the bed. Vaguely he could see her naked form. With her, John Bold told himself, there would be none of the histrionics of the white virgin bride on her wedding night. He got in beside her, she gave the faintest of shudders. After a moment or two he placed his hand on her breast and felt her tense, that was all. Her breathing was regular and shallow. God damnit, he told himself, here I am about to furrow her and not a word is spoken, not a caress given. Angrily, he thrust himself at her and pressed her lips to his. Their teeth clashed awkwardly until she opened her mouth and he pressed his tongue inside. Perhaps involuntarily, her arms slipped around his neck and closed at the nape in the first gesture of any kind that she had given ever since they had met. But now nature was beginning to take its course and suddenly he was very excited. It was nearly two months since he had possessed a woman. His hands were everywhere. On her

63

breasts, her hair, her belly, the tops of her legs. By now she was panting too. As if of its own volition, her stomach started to move rythmically in and out. She was becoming excited! Firmly, but gently, John placed his hand between her shaven thighs. His nostrils were assailed by the scent of saffron and something else – that of a woman on heat. He hesitated no longer. His finger went into that naked cleft. It was moist and hot. 'Yes?', he said. It was not a question but a statement. She made no reply, but slowly and definitely her legs started to spread in anticipation.

Only once during the hours that followed, did he glance down at her in the faint light from outside. She looked like some wild animal that had been done violence to. He felt a sudden deep sense of shame. Yet he knew he had only forced her to betray her true nature. Covering her with kisses, he'd wanted to make her blind, deaf to reason, feeling only animal heat. And it had worked, or so he thought. He had felt her arch under him, legs clasped around his back, her breath coming in shallow gasps. She was groaning and lathered in sweat, then wild and panting like a crazy woman. Suddenly he realized that he was no longer the master. *She* was in charge. Yet soon he knew she would sleep and then he must be gone. He would need all his strength for what was soon to come.

As she lapsed into exhaustion and slept, he gathered up his boots, food parcel and clothes and hoped that the princess would not suffer for her negligence. He had planned to strike her unconscious so that she could prove to Po and his master that she had been powerless to stop the escaper, but he had been unable to do so. Swiftly he drew his socks on over his boots. That way he could move through the house almost noiselessly. He crept to the main door of the upper floor. As he had suspected, it was not locked. Unlike European houses, there were few locks or bolts in Asiatic places. Keeping to the shadows of the stairwell, he started to descend to the ground floor. But there was a sound coming from behind the door to his immediate left: then he grinned as he recognized it for the sound of someone urinating into a thunder mug.

64

Momentarily he wondered if the chamber pot was made of gold, too, just like everything else seemed to be in this place.

In another three hours it would be dawn and by then he had to be long gone. During his night-long search he had been unable to make out a sentinel. But if there were one on guard he could be positioned outside the main portal. Inch by inch he eased it open. The next minute he had done it. He was free and undiscovered! Confidence and hope flooded through his body as he stepped into the grounds only to freeze the next moment. Now he knew why the golden cage had been without sentinels; this hulking guard dog sufficed in their stead.

Slowly the beast lowered its snout, ears pricked. It bared its ugly yellow teeth and Bold heard the first low growl commence. He felt his blood run cold, and gripped his knife even more tightly. What had Old Boney once said; 'the best defence is attack'? He had to get the bastard before it got him and there was only one way to silence it when he did. He prayed fervently that the cur was a male.

Next moment he launched himself forward in a shallow dive. The beast was caught off guard, surprised. When it jerked back onto its hind legs, as Bold had hoped, his left hand shot out, sought and found the animal's penis. Without hesitation he twisted it – *hard*. In the same instant that the beast yelped with pain and fell to its side, Bold plunged home the knife. Suddenly the dog went limp. Even as it did so, John Bold woke to his new danger. Of course, the killer dog would have a handler – someone to fetch him at the end of the night when his guard duties were at an end.

About a hundred yards away in the velvet shadows he saw the dark figure moving. But it was already too late. The man had cried something in Burmese and the very next instant he raised his musket. *Crack*! Scarlet flame stabbed the darkness. A ball whizzed by John's head and slammed into a tree not a yard away, showering him with splinters. Tiny yellow oil lights flickered on everywhere.

The alarm had been raised. The hunt for John Bold had commenced.

3

John Bold lay in the kalai grass, hands pressed to his eyes. They were red-rimmed with fatigue and hurt like the devil. After a night and a day on the run, he was lathered with sweat and his clothes were tattered, ripped by the thorns he'd encountered everywhere when he had been forced to plunge into the deeper jungle to escape his pursuers.

Now he lay there gratefully, catching his breath and trying to ignore the myriad mosquitoes which tortured him unmercifully. Already the area around his eyes had been bitten so badly that the flesh had puffed up and his eyes were mere slits. At least the mosquitoes signalled their approach with their infernal buzzing, but the midges dropped out of the air silently in clouds, and within seconds would cover him with bites. They were damnable. But despite his weariness, John remained fairly confident. The night before he had set his course by the Southern Cross and had proceeded in an easterly direction heading for the Irrawaddy, where he hoped to find the boat he needed. He also desperately needed water. The patch of sky he could manage to see through the jungle canopy above was beginning to darken. Soon, he guessed, night would fall once more with the dramatic suddenness of the tropics. He welcomed it, for in the distance he could hear the faint calls of the pursuers who had found his track. The jungle foliage always muted the sound and there was no wind to carry it, either. The men who were after him could have been a mile away or a mere hundred yards.

The sense of smell of the Burmese was acute. Just as he could identify them by their unique body odour, they could scent him as a white man from a long way off. So once he started moving again and began to sweat more heavily, they'd smell him. Whereas in the thick jungle where he now found himself, it was exceedingly difficult to see more than five yards ahead. Here his body odour was less likely to give him away. Another half an hour or so and it would be dark. Then the Burmese would give up their chase till the morning, for they were deadly scared of the animals of the jungle. He knew they would build large fires and squat close to them, shivering more with fear than the sudden night cold, and wait for dawn. Just then his nostrils were assailed by a sickly-sweet smell, and he forgot his pursuers. It was one he had experienced many times before ever since he had first occasioned it as an eighteen-year old ensign at the Battle of Waterloo. The smell of death! Curious, he crawled forward a few yards into the undergrowth. There he saw it, the remains of what appeared to be a small deer. All that was left now was the head, a bunch of splintered bones and a few dry rags of flesh attached to the hide. It was not alone. Just beyond he spotted drag marks in the dry powdery earth leading to a dead boar. It was a huge creature, covered in hard black bristle, the flesh still intact.

Some instinct made him look up; why was there not a single vulture in sight? They and the ants were always first to scent death. He had his dead Irish father's feeling for the unknown; that Celtic sixth sense, which had saved him more than once in the past. Now he felt that old force overcome him once more. Involuntarily, despite the sweltering heat, he shivered. There was something out there.

Like a conjuror's illusion it appeared silently from a patch of trees. A huge tigress, perhaps six foot in length or more, its muscles rolling beneath its loose striped coat! He caught his breath. In all his years in India he had never been so close to such a beast even when out hunting. Now he was virtually unarmed. Even when he had become an old man, John Bold would always remember those green eyes as they stared him out unwinkingly. That gaze epitomized power and naked cruelty.

He waited for the inevitable. But nothing happened. The tigress simply gazed at him as if he were part of the jungle scenery, then stalked on and past him to a spot further up the ditch. But his ordeal was not yet over. Hardly had he praised God for his good fortune when there was a great roar and another tiger bounded into view – a magnificent male. Only as he waited for it to pounce did he suddenly realise what was going on. *The two beasts were mating*! He had been caught up unwittingly in their rituals. He remembered how old hunting hands back in Bengal had told him that female tigers went into some kind of dazed, unseeing trance when they were on heat, forgetting everything but the male sex.

The male tiger certainly didn't seem at all dazed. He was getting more and more frenzied by the moment and rather than interrupt his courtship, John Bold deemed it expedient to continue his trek through the jungle after all.

By nightfall on the second day of his escape, John Bold had just about reached the Irrawaddy. The meeting with the giant tigers, frightening as it was, had been of some value. It had scared off his pursuers for a while. For hours now he had not heard their cries back and forth and he reasoned that once they had heard the roaring of the male beast, they had gone to earth immediately, probably surrounding themselves with their great fires and a stockade made of pointed bamboo.

The approach to the great river brought with it other dangers. The jungle had begun to thin out, to be replaced by paddies and large vegetable gardens. Here and there he could glimpse the thatched circles of small hamlets which meant human habitation. Not only was the Irrawaddy the easiest way of movement and transportation within the remote rugged country, but it also provided a source of livelihood other than agriculture for the peasants, namely fishing. Now weary and filthy as he was, his exposed flesh sunburned and sore, he would have to keep absolutely alert if he did not want to walk right into the arms of some waiting village watchman.

Just before dawn Bold was in sight of the great sweep of the river itself, nearly a mile broad at this point, but still yellow and sluggish – with bright red sandbanks sticking out here and there, indicating that the water was quite shallow. He looked longingly at the reaches closest to him. He would dearly love to plunge his wounded body in that cool water and then drink his fill until his stomach was full and distended. But that was too dangerous now. He would have to content himself with what rain-water he could find lodged in the fronds of the surrounding palms.

While he surveyed the river and made his plans, he cast around for a good day-time hiding place. He had only this day to find his boat, whatever food he might be able to steal and above all a supply of water. For the chase would soon commence once more.

He spotted a pile of volcanic rocks, heavily bearded with moss, surrounded by clumps of azalea, merging into the bamboo which clicked and sighed every time they were struck by any kind of breeze. 'That's it,' he said to himself in the manner of lonely men who converse with themselves. 'Any movement I might make will be taken for the wind in the bamboos. Besides their tubes'll contain water.' Five minutes later he had safely ensconced in the circle of bamboo and azalea, lying full-length on one of the rocks, and able to spend the next hours watching the comings and goings on the Irrawaddy.

As he had surmised, it was a busy place. All morning great loose rafts of teak were propelled along the lazy yellow water by teams of half-naked sweating coolies, bending over their curved poles. In between, fishermen, weighed down under huge conical straw hats, threw their nets into the water – drawing them out later filled with the wriggling silver sheen of their catch. More than once tiny boys with distended bellies herded water buffalo into the shallows and washed the caked ordure from their flanks, throwing handfuls of river-water at the cracked hides to drive away the flies, making a great giggling game of it all. How Bold envied them!

By noon, he had established that somewhere just around the next bend, out of sight, there must be a small fishing village. For it was from there that the fishing boats – simple trunks of teak hollowed out by fire and axe – came, as well as the boy buffalo herders. If he were going to find a boat, it would be there, he concluded. But he reasoned, too, that the news of his escape *might* already have reached this far and that the Lord of the White Elephant and the Golden Foot *might* have given orders to the unknown villagers to guard their craft at night. How this news might have been passed from Rangoon to the remote village he did not know. The Burmese, he thought, would possess no heliograph and of course they would know nothing of the newfangled telegraph introduced by Herr Reuter of Aachen. Yet two hours later, as he lay in the shade of the bamboo, he learned that his fears had been correct.

Later he would not be able to recall what had first warned him, but instantly he was fully alert, his fatigue forgotten. *Someone was coming!* And, from the noise being made, there was more than one of them. . . .

4

Sweeney, who thought he had long forgotten the 'Oud Sod', the holy water and all the mumbo-jumbo that went with being Irish and Catholic, crossed himself in the darkness for the first time in years. It was the only kind of good luck that he could wish himself. For now he was about to commit a military crime which would warrant a general court martial and probably the firing squad if he were found guilty. The ageing Lieutenant was under no delusions about that. Colonel Lord Cavendish would have him dancing a jig on the gibbet, as they'd say back in his boyhood County Sligo, as soon as look at him.

He flashed a look to where the C.O. had had the mess erected, a couple of tents on the highest point of the island so that the officers could capture whatever breeze came wafting in from the sea. All was quiet now. There were no lights. Sweeney wasn't surprised. Cavendish and his cronies had put away at least a case of iced champagne after the dinner, and there had been plenty of port and madeira, too. The lot of them had been well in their cups when he had excused himself and that had been two hours ago, at least.

He nodded to his fellow conspirators, 'All right, me boyos,' he whispered, 'start getting the men to the longboats and tell 'em to button up their lips and make no noise. There'll be a bottle of grog for each man once we reach the *Diana*, as long as they don't give the game away.' He grinned in spite of the tension. 'And that should keep 'em quiet. Yer average Tommy Atkins would sell his own mother for a whole bottle of grog.'

While Sweeney watched, trying to silence the nerve which ticked anxiously at his left temple, the hundred-odd men who had volunteered to come with him and his fellow conspirators filed one by one towards the waiting

72

boats, which jogged up and down on the surf. They marched through the white sand barefoot, boots slung around their backs, arms and equipment muffled with old rags so that they did not clink and give the game away. Impatiently the swabs manning the boats hissed that the soldiers should hurry. They sensed that there was someone wrong about this midnight embarkation, and unlike the John company's Army, the Royal Navy still flogged its men brutally. They wanted no trouble, whatever was going on, and asked no questions.

Sweeney threw a last glance at Cavendish's tented headquarters. All was silent up there. Suddenly his face relaxed into a soft smile. He'd give a year's pay, he told himself, to see the look on his lordship's silly face on the morrow when he discovered that a quarter of his regiment had disappeared into the blue. Then he turned and allowed himself to be helped into the longboat by the sailors eager to be off.

On the hillock above the beach, General Campbell, minus his furry bonnet, his old plaid wrapped around his shoulders to keep off the chill wind blowing in from the sea, watched the boats as they rowed out to the dark shape of the *Diana*, smoke already pouring from her funnel. It struck the Scot that there was no rhyme or reason to life. His grandfather had run before Johnnie Wade and his redcoats at Cullodon to swear afterwards he would 'nair sup a dish o' tee with no Sassenach' ever again. His father had tossed a coin, after the English banned the kilt in Scotland, to decide whether he should go 'o'er the water' to France and serve there as a mercenary or join the new regiment formed by the hated English – the Black Watch. The coin had decided he'd join the Black Watch. Now here was he Archie Campbell, the grandbairn of that angry veteran after the defeat of Scotland's hopes at the Battle of Cullodon, wearing the kilt and commanding a British Army. What logical purpose was there to that?

It was the same with Lieutenant Sweeney and his company of deserters. Sweeney had never had the money to purchase promotion and was ending a career to be faced with penury and possibly the workhouse in an ungrateful England; he was now taking a terrible risk upon himself. For what? A promotion in India, if he lived long enough to be granted it.

Campbell shook his grizzled head and then grinned as out in the bay the *Diana*'s paddlewheels started to creak and groan, heralding the departure of the old tea-kettle. Of course, he'd deny any knowledge of what had happened this night – for a while at least. Only once they had sailed, would he tell his lordship what he had done, for then there would be no turning back. Cavendish would simply have to put a good face on it. Naturally he would harbour a grudge and would report everything to his uncle, the Governor-General, when they returned to Calcutta. But as Campbell had told himself before, if the Army were victorious the 'crime' would be overlooked. If it were defeated, nothing would matter anyway. Satisfied that he had done all he could and full of the old Calvinist belief of his dour Highland forefathers that all was predestined, good or evil, he drew his plaid closer and watched as the *Diana* slipped anchor and began to move out into the moonlit bay. He watched her just until she merged with the horizon, then he turned and stumped back across the sand to his own tent. For better or worse, they were on their way.

Some two hundred miles or so away on the other side of that same sea, John Bold also realized that there was an inevitability about fate. There was nothing you could do really to affect it. At first his hopes had slumped to zero when he had heard a patrol coming along the river bank. 'Your goose is cooked now, Bold,' a hard little voice had commented inside his head.

They had come towards him, chattering loudly, taking no precautions, and by straining his ears he had decided there were five of them and armed, too, because he could hear the regular clink of their weapons as they moved through the undergrowth with difficulty. For a few

74

moments he had panicked. They seemed so confident, as if they knew he was here somewhere and he was theirs for the taking. Lying full-length in the bamboo he could hear his own heart thumping and had tried to bury himself deeper into the ground. His eyes narrowed to slits, he watched them. In a careless sort of way, they appeared to be searching the ground, occasionally crying to one another in a bored manner. They might well have been a bunch of schoolboys sent out to pick wild flowers to press between the leaves of their crammer. Bold concentrated on the last one, who bore an ancient flintlock as he lagged further behind the others. Then Bold realized why. Just as the first of the little search party disappeared from sight, this man squatted in a fold in the ground and laid his flintlock on the grass next to him. He was going to relieve his bowels.

It came to Bold with the total clarity of a vision that this lone native was his saviour; his way out. His clothing would provide him with the cover he needed if he were going to approach the native village tonight and steal a boat. In the dusk and if he stooped a little – for he was much taller than the average Burmese – he might well be taken for one of their own kind. Almost before he knew it, Bold inched his way through the undergrowth to where the unsuspecting native strained, a handful of leaves already at the ready in his left hand. Crouched like that, he was easy meat.

Bold decided to rely upon his own muscular power. He'd have to strangle any cry the native might attempt to make right at the start. When he was merely yards away, he dived forward and the native turned, startled. Too late! Already Bold had his arm around his neck and was exerting all his strength. He thrust his knee into the small of the native's back and tugged until he felt no resistance. Bold relaxed his grip. The man was dead.

In the hamlet itself there was little going on. The half-naked children had all vanished to bed. Here and there in the raised houses, supported by wooden piles, there was a curl of grey smoke arising in the still night air from the cooking braziers. A couple of skinny dogs slouched about, too, but they remained close to the houses and Bold guessed that if they were like Indian dogs, they were too badly treated to howl at any stranger and raise the alarm.

In the end he decided that he would have to aim for the boat closest to the river. If the alarm *were* raised, he wanted to be in the water and gone before any pursuit could gather pace. That decided, he began to look around for some food. The chickens he had seen under the raised huts were out of the question. He knew from his youth in England, what a racket chickens could kick up when their nest were being raided. So he fixed on some of the fish hanging on the lines just outside the village drying in the sun, And there was a well handily situated to the edge of the hamlet.

He flashed one last look at the darkened hamlet and then he emerged from the jungle, the single-shot flintlock at the ready. Cautiously he started with the fish – some kind of sole which smelled to high heaven, but when he took a hesitant bite from one of them it tasted all right. Carefully he stowed a bundle of them inside the native shirt, then moved on to the well. There were several pots lying around and he picked one which he judged might hold a gallon. All was perfectly still. Gingerly he played out the rope which held the bucket, then hauled it up and filled his jug. Next he headed for the primitive little boat which he had singled out for himself. It had a paddle and a rudimentary sail too, furled at the bottom. With a lurch and the sound of sucking sand, as if the ground was reluctant to relax its hold, he started to push it through the sand. He dare not lose the momentum, for one second.

Suddenly Bold's heart gave a leap of joy: the boat was no longer so heavy, its bow was in the water. He could have shouted out loud at the discovery. Instead, he gave another hefty shove and felt the little craft rock as it bobbed on the surface of the water. *He had done it!*

The shot rang out with startling clarity. He actually heard the angry ball whiz by his head and strike the water a few yards away kicking up an angry white plume. He spun round to see a bunch of men had emerged from the forest, perhaps some hundred yards away, carrying with them a bundle which he instantly guessed was the body of the native he had murdered in the undergrowth. There were about a dozen of them standing there in the faint light cast by the stars, and two of them were armed with flintlocks. Bold cursed eloquently. Already the man who had fired was hurriedly reloading, ramming down the charge while the other one with arms was taking aim. Once he'd fired, Bold guessed the others would rush him with their spears and swords. With one and the same movement, fear lending speed to his actions he kicked the little boat further into the water, praying that the current would seize it and snatched up his own plundered flint-lock.

He fired instinctively. The butt of the ancient weapon slammed into his shoulder. But at that range he couldn't miss. A flash of brilliant scarlet, a burst of black smoke, and the ball was hurtling towards the man about to retali-ate. It caught him in the chest and seemed to burst him apart splattering blood over the others. With a shrill scream of agony, the man was propelled backwards as if punched by an invisible fist.

Next moment all was noise and confusion. The patrol dropped to the ground, shouting angrily, while over in the village little flickering lights were ignited everywhere. In a minute they would all be streaming out of their houses and the patrol would recover their courage.

John Bold did not wait for that to happen. Dropping the flintlock to the sand, he pelted waist-deep into the river and flung himself into a shallow dive as another ball came howling across the surface of the sand. Next moment he was swimming all out to catch up with his little craft.

5

There was no denying it, Sweeney told himself as the young officer walked down the length of his squadron, Senior Ensign Hodgson was a darkie. His name was English, of course, but the jet black hair, the dark eyes and the un-English gestures told the infantryman that the acting commander of Bold's Horse had plenty of the tarbrush in him. Not that that mattered much Sweeney reflected, as Hodgson started to come to the end of his inspection of his Indian troopers, the officer had the look of a fighter and Sweeney had noted the sabre scars on his right hand and arm, the sure sign of a cavalryman who had been in battle.

Sweeney wiped his damp brow and stared out to the east, but the blue horizon remained obstinately empty, as the *Diana* ploughed steadily through the sea trailing a great cloud of black smoke behind her. But he had had a word with a master just after finishing the morning inspection of his own company and Captain Hughes, a Welshman as dark as the coal that filled the ship's bunkers, had promised they'd sight the coast of Burma within the next twelve hours. Sweeney frowned as he thought about the landing that wasn't going to be easy. There were only sufficient longboats and naval crews to man them for his own company of foot. Hodgson and his native troopers would have to swim their mounts ashore and from his past experiences at Dunkirk and Walcheren, Sweeney knew that horses sometimes panicked when they were faced with heavy surf or waves.

'Riding Master,' Hodgson's keen, clear-cut voice interrupted his thoughts, as he prepared to dismiss the morning parade, 'will you carry on, please?'

Riding Master Sergeant 'Fornication and Rum' Jones, known throughout the Army of Madras for his bible-thumping and his evangelism – that is when he wasn't drunk – came to a parody of the position of attention. For the little white-haired Welshman was hopelessly bow-legged after decades of training cavalry horses. He snapped up a terrific salute though and swung round on the squadron's *Rissaldar*. '*Rissaldar sahib*', he called, 'dismiss the men!'

Hodgson removed his shako and wiped his brow as he approached the infantry officer. 'God, isn't it hot, Lieutenant,' he sighed, 'and it's not yet noon. How I could go a chotta peg with heaps of ice in it!'

Sweeney told himself that at least the young half-breed drank – unlike most of his native cavalry. That was another sign in his favour, for Sweeney had an Irishman's distrust of anyone who did not drink – and drink hard. 'It'll get hotter no doubt, Ensign. And that Welsh skipper up there'll allow no hard stuff till after sundown. He's another one of yer bible-thumpers like yon sergeant of yourn.'

Hodgson gave him an easy grin, and Sweeney warmed to him. He wasn't a bad fellow at all – for a darkie. 'A damn good NCO, though,' Hodgson said, 'and riding master. Her certainly puts my chaps through their paces. But God, he must be old! Look at that cropped head of his. Obviously he goes back to the days when the British Army still wore wigs.' Then he dismissed the bow-legged riding master. 'Hm,' he broached the new subject a little hesitantly – after all Sweeney was a good quarter of a century older than he – 'I hear we should be approaching our destination within the next twelve hours.' And when Sweeney nodded, he added, 'Well, Lieutenant, we have a rough plan from General Campbell. The Horse will go in first and penetrate inland, while your foot follows and takes up positions further back on the beach. That's the way I understand it.'

Again Sweeney nodded, wondering where the young Ensign was leading, but he said nothing.

'It's the question of co-ordination, you see, Lieutenant,' Hodgson said a little nervous. He knew the average British

79

officer's attitude to 'half-breeds' or 'yallahs' as they sometimes called them contemptuously.

'You mean, who shall have charge of the whole operation?' Sweeney put it bluntly.

'Yes, exactly,' Hodgson admitted, grateful that the subject was out in the open, for he knew his late CO Major Bold would never have subjected himself to the orders of a foot-slogger. The Major had had pretty firm opinions on the role of irregular cavalry such as his own squadron.

Sweeney gave the embarrassed younger officer a rough smile, showing the gaps in his rotten teeth. 'I don't think, Ensign, *anyone* should be in overall control. Once we've co-ordinated what each of us is to do, then I feel it's up to each one of us to carry out his task in any manner he thinks fit.' He saw the look of pleasure his words had given Hodgson and said, 'After all, it should be a matter of twenty-four or thirty-six hours at the most till General Campbell and the main force catch up with us, and then both of us will come under the General's orders once more. I don't think we can do very much wrong in a day, do you, Ensign?

'Of course, Lieutenant,' Hodgson agreed eagerly, obviously very much relieved that Sweeney had placed no objections in the way of his squadron operating independently. For he intended to do what he thought the CO would have done in his shoes. He would penetrate as deep inland as possible. As soon as he bumped into serious trouble, he would begin to withdraw *slowly*, trying to stave off the enemy attacks until Campbell was firmly established on the beach. He was sure those would have been poor Major Bold's tactics.

Sweeney seemed able to read his mind, for he said: 'I haven't enough men to cover a very wide front, Hodgson, so the more space you can cover the better. It will give the foot more of a buffer when the fighting gets started. The widest possible sweep with the men available to you, is what I'd like to see.'

'You shall have it, Lieutenant Sweeney,' Hodgson agreed happily. 'For one day at least, you and I will have our independence. Let us make the most of playing generals, eh?'

Sweeney smiled, carried away by the darkie's enthusiasm. 'Now then, my lad,' he said lowering his voice in case the Welsh bible-thumper on the bridge of the *Diana* might hear, 'What about a drop of the hard stuff now in my cabin. There'll be no ice, I'm afraid, but it'll take the coating off'n yer teeth.' He displayed his own blackened ruins, as if to explain the power of the rotgut he usually drank. Hodgson grinned back at him, revealing a perfect set of brilliant white teeth and whispered in the same conspiratorial fashion, 'Lead on McDuff . . . lead on. . . .

The two officers would not have been so sanguine about the success of their combined operation in Burma, if they had realised the difficulties General Campbell was currently facing off the Andaman Isles. As he had anticipated, Lord Cavendish had kicked up a terrible fuss when he discovered that one fourth of his battalion had disappeared overnight. His face red with fury, he had come charging into Campbell's tent without so much as a by-your-leave and had immediately accused the General of being party to the disappearance of Lieutenant Sweeney's company. Campbell's mien had remained composed, 'I pray you to calm yourself, Colonel,' he had said coldly. 'It is not customary for colonels of foot in the British Army to force their way into a general's presence without permission or through proper channels.'

'A fig for your permissions and proper channels!' Cavendish had snorted and at that moment Campbell half-expected the Colonel to stamp his foot like a petulant child. Cavendish didn't. Instead he said: 'This must be reported to the Governor-General at once. There must be an inquiry. I demand it!'

Campbell looked up at him, bleak-faced. 'You may demand as much as you like, Colonel Cavendish. But there will be no report to the Governor-General or inquiry. We have no time for such trivia now. I am in charge here and it is my word – my word alone – which counts. Your connections are in India and London, but they are far away now and play no rôle in my plans. Do you understand that, sir?'

'No,' Cavendish blurted out, tears of impotent rage in his eyes. 'I refuse categorically to serve under you or obey your orders. My battalion will not sail until I have been given an explanation for what happened last night.'

Campbell's stance remained unchanged. 'Then, sir if you refuse to take my orders to embark your men, I shall relieve you of your command.'

'But my father paid for that regiment!' Cavendish stared at him aghast, as if he could not believe the evidence of his own ears.

'Your regiment, sir,' Campbell thundered in return 'still belongs to the British Army, whatever you or your father might think to the contrary! It consists of human beings who are expected to risk their lives for three shillings and sixpence a week, and what food and clothing you care to provide for them . . . and from what I hear, sir, there is precious little of that. So pray let me have no more of *your* regiment and what *your* father paid for it! If you are not prepared to sail and fight with the foot, well then, you can stay here if you wish and I shall personally hand over the command of the regiment to your second-in-command. I *am* making myself clear, am I not?'

Cavendish looked at Campbell and felt it would be wiser to say nothing. He had nodded mutely and had gone out, murder in his heart. After he had done so, Campbell leaned back on the hard wooden camp stool, telling himself he had made a mortal enemy who would betray him – do him down – at the first possible opportunity. But at least Cavendish's foot would embark on the morrow at least, that was the main thing.

Cavendish's regiment did indeed embark and this time Campbell made it perfectly clear to a sullen Cavendish that he did not want the men cooped up and baking in the stinking hold for twenty-four hours on end. Every four hours they were to be allowed on deck in company strength to stretch their legs and cool off in the fresher air topside. Each man was to receive two bottles of ale a day, and there was to be constant access to seawater for washing. Numbly Cavendish had agreed and Campbell had told himself that with a bit of luck the vital regiment of foot would emerge from the hold when they finally made landfall, fresh and ready for action.

Yet it seemed that Campbell's luck had run out. For hardly had the little fleet lifted anchor when the sailing ships were completely becalmed. There was not enough wind for tacking and within the hour, the fuming ships' captain had to signal a worried General Campbell that there seemed no hope of wind this day. In despair, he turned to Captain Marryat of the *Larne* on which he was sailing and asked in his broadest Scots, 'An' yon wind, Captain, whur's yon wind?'

And Captain Marryat had shaken his head almost sadly and answered, 'I'm afraid all we can do, General is to whistle for it.'

Almost as if he were speaking to himself, Campbell whispered, 'But if we canna catch up with the *Diana* and she lands those puir laddies, they'll be slaughtered outright. . . . '

Captain Marryat turned away hastily, for the General's head had fallen to his chest. But before he had done so, the naval officer had caught the glint of tears and he would have sworn the old warrior was crying.

As the *Diana* anchored that same evening, the sun was already sinking fast, losing its fire, leaving all the watchers grateful for the cooler air. By now the sea had lost its brassy shimmer. Already it was beginning to take on colours, blue merging into green, green into grey and shading imperceptibly to the far horizon. In thirty minutes or so it would be pitch-black. On the deck the officers searched the horizon with their spy glasses and telescopes. Although it was difficult to make out anything clearly, there was no doubt about it – that smudge to the east was land. They were off the coast of enemy country. They had arrived at their destination, and according to the captain of the steamship, it would only be a couple of

83

hours before they were in a position to land troops. It was up to the Army now: when did they want to land?

Both Sweeney and Hodgson were undecided. They knew that they must find a beach that sloped gently upwards, if it sloped at all. For both the foot and the cavalry would be stopped by anything resembling a cliff. Besides a cliff, defended by even a handful of the enemy, would present an unsurmountable obstacle. For a while they considered trying to land in the delta of the Irrawaddy, going ashore on the right bank, the one closest to Rangoon. But after some thought they rejected that possibility. As Hodgson pointed out, 'If any place is likely to be populated, Lieutenant, it will be the river bank and we don't want the alarm to be raised as soon as we land, do we?'

'Yes of course you're right, Ensign,' Sweeney had agreed. 'We of the foot want to lie doggo as long as possible without discovery – at least until the General and the main body arrive.'

As it grew steadily darker and the *Diana*, its paddle-wheels churning water that was becoming increasingly more yellow, came closer to the enemy coast, they had still not given their instructions to the Captain. Though they had decided they would land at dawn before whoever fished these remote waters was abroad. Steadily the two officers became more frustrated. As Sweeney said, a little bitterly, 'Why in any other place, ye'd at least have a chart to show where everything is and what the ground looks like, but even the Captain of this newfangled tea-kettle only has something that might have been made by Marco Polo when he first came this way donkey's years ago.'

Hodgson would have laughed at Sweeney's outburst on any other occasion, but not now. His responsibility for his own men and the task given him by General Campbell weighed too heavily. He knew what the other officers of the invasion force thought of him: some damned half-breed of a counter-jumper whom the John Company in its infinite wisdom had placed in an officer's uniform. He was sure that some would dearly love to see him fail, but he was determined not to and the first essential for later success was to find a suitable spot to swim his horses and men ashore.

It was while the two officers studied the shoreline, faces set and anxious, that the lookout perched on a makeshift crow's nest sang out, 'Object to starboard, gentlemen.'

Hurriedly the two of them focused their glasses and could just make out what first appeared to be a log, tossing in the waves some three quarters of a mile away. 'Probably a tree trunk of something,' Sweeney commented, then he stopped short and focused once more.

Hodgson did the same. As his eyesight was keener than that of the older man, he was first to make the discovery. 'It isn't, Lieutenant!' he said with sudden excitement, tinged with fear. Did what he had just seen indicate that they had been discovered already? 'That log's got a little sail in front of it!'

'Why, damnit,' Sweeney agreed, 'you're right. . . . '

Bold's first night in the stolen craft had passed quickly. The current had taken him down the Irrawaddy, mercifully sweeping him by the other craft plying their trade in the broad delta, for he had only the crude paddle to steer with. Just before dawn, while he had still been covered by the velvet darkness of the tropical night, he had been swept out to sea. By sunrise he was alone, a mere black dot in an infinite waste of brilliant blue, seemingly the only man left alive in the whole world.

The next day had been terrible. An eternity had drifted by under a remorseless blazing sun, as he had lain in the little craft in a stupor of exhaustion, both of the body and mind. At times he had seen everything through what appeared to be a mist so that all around him seemed hazy and shrouded. By the end of his first long hot day, he had eaten one of the fish he had stolen and tossed the rest away in disgust – for the sun-dried and salted fish had given him an intolerable thirst, which couldn't be quenched as he had used most of his water. All he could do was to dip his face in seawater which made his blistered face sting like hell.

By noon of the second day his eyes were glued shut, and he became aware of a terrible drowsiness stealing over him – a low, creeping paralysis of the mind and body which he knew heralded death. Yet although he knew he was dying, John Bold did not seem to care. He would be glad of the relief that death would bring. Then it would all be over and he would be free of his raging thirst.

Now it was almost dark and he was still alive. From far away, he seemed to hear someone calling his name very faintly. Even Death refused to come to aid him! In a dream-like fashion, he felt something descend upon his body and tighten round his waist, and then he was rising through the air as if by magic. He could hear speech in tongues which he understood. It was not Burmese. Slowly he began to realize that he was not going to die after all.

A hand nudged his neck. He raised his head obediently. Something deliciously cool and thirst-quenching trickled down his parched throat. For the first time in hours, he could actually move his swollen tongue.

'He's coming round', someone said in what he thought was an Irish accent.

And then a familiar Welsh voice cried in joy, 'Praise the Lord, 'tis like Lazarus raised from the death. PRAISE THE LORD!'

John Bold peered upwards and for a moment he was able to focus his eyes. 'Fornication . . . and Rum Jones,' he said weakly. 'Is, is it really you?' Then his head fell to one side and he was gone.

6

It was a day later.

The balding little brown Indian *feldschar*, Gopta, attached to the expedition had worked wonders with the exhausted officer in that period of time. As soon as Bold had slept for eight hours, he had awoken him and commenced curing his various ailments, using a mixture of Western and Oriental medicine. The eyes had come first. He had soon drained the puffiness out of them with his leeches. Within the hour Bold had been able to see out of them once more, though the cure had resulted in the appearance of two black eyes.

The fat Indian doctor who talked to himself all the time while he worked – in his own tongue and broken English – also applied himself to Bold's legs, scratched, torn and covered with insect bites from the time spent in the jungle. He had bound them in bandages, smeared with what appeared to be a soft plaster of Paris and waited till it had semi-hardened. Once that had taken place, he had peeled off the bandages to reveal to a somewhat startled Bold the myriad ticks, bugs, worms and insects which had been drawn out of his limbs.

Of course, the food and drinks which Hodgson, Jones and his troopers had fed to their CO at intervals as soon as he came to had their usual disastrous effect. 'Thin shits – but no blood, good,' Gopta had opined, after peering into the Major's thunder-mug. 'Still we must cure. Otherwise bloody nuisance.' He had beamed at a groaning Bold, whose stomach seemed to be on fire, and within fifteen minutes the patient was completely naked, touching his toes, while Gopta pumped some kind of aromatic smoke up his rear by means of a bellows. Surprisingly enough the cure worked and by that dusk Bold found himself well enough to summon an officers' conference in the

Captain's cabin, which the Welshman had placed at his disposal until he recovered.

In between bouts of sickness and Gopta's 'cures', Bold had learned enough of the expedition and its aims to have come to some decisions of his own. Weak as he still was, he realized that he must assume command of the assault force. For he was the only one present who knew the terrain and the current situation in the enemy's capital. Others might have to engage in the actual fighting, but he would give the orders and he made that quite clear right from the start. As he lay in his bunk, with the oil-lamp swinging back and forth over his head and Gopta standing somewhat possessively at his side, he declared, 'Gentlemen, I have taken over command and I will say this from the outset. We shall land not on the coast out there,' he indicated the direction in which the *Diana* was sailing, 'No gentlemen, there is only one spot where we can launch our assault – and that is Rangoon itself.'

There was a gasp of surprise from his listeners.

Bold had expected it and waited patiently till the noise died away. He watched their faces, yellow and hollowed-out in the flickering light cast by the oil-lamp. They might well have been the skulls of dead men and he told himself a little sorrowfully that before many moons had passed some of them would be. 'Now why Rangoon?' he asked and answered his own question. He told them how he had seen great hordes of armed warriors passing north through the city during his imprisonment, and how the Burmese ruler had asked him to guide his expedition into India against Calcutta.' It is clear, therefore, gentlemen, that this so-called Lord of the White Elephant and Golden Foot has directed his army to take the same route that your General Campbell has rejected. It is clear, too, that Rangoon has been stripped of enemy troops in order that they may take part in that invasion through the Arracan.'

'That may be, sir,' Sweeney objected. 'But I assume yon Rangoon is a fair-sized place. How can a company of foot and a squadron of horse hold a capital city, Major?'

'I shall tell you, Lieutenant. Of course they can't.'

'Can't!' someone echoed.

'Naturally not, but we are not going to hold the *whole* of Rangoon. I know one single spot which dominates it. With that in our hands, we need not attempt to take the capital as such. Far from it, we shall be masters of the place as it is.'

'And what is that place, sir?' Hodgson asked, his relief that Bold was now back in command all too obvious.

'Why Ensign, no less a place than the Golden Pagoda.'

Hodgson whistled softly through his teeth. 'I've heard of it,' he said.

'Me, too, sir,' Sweeney added heartily. 'They say it's made of solid gold. What a great fine place to loot that will be!'

'It is a kind of church,' Bold said softly.

Sweeney grinned. 'Ay, but a heathen one, sir and they don't count, do they now?'

Bold shook his head in mock wonder and continued. 'My plan is to sail up the estuary right into Rangoon itself. The Golden Pagoda lies to the east of the city. Therefore it is close to the water. The aim would be to land, attack and capture the place in a *coup de main*. It would all have to be done swiftly and decisively. We have neither the time, the troops nor the resources for any prolonged fighting in the streets leading to the Golden Pagoda. Is that clear?'

There was a mumble of assent from the listening officers, as Bold allowed them a few moments to absorb his daring plan. He knew nothing of what was going through their minds, but as he watched them he thought again of England – which he had not seen for ten years now and probably never would see again. There, the last of the February snow would probably have vanished by now and the people would be looking forward to spring and the new greenness. What quiet, pleasant lives they all lived there! Even a dweller in London's teeming slums could never visualize a life such as that led by these officers, full of bloodshed, violence and sudden death. This night these men were planning to add another large chunk to the greatest empire the world had ever seen. But back in the centre of that empire, no one knew of them or cared a fig for them. If they had to die soon, they would do so unknown and unsung.

'What then, sir?' Sweeney posed the question they were all thinking, 'after we've captured the Golden Pagoda?'

'We dig in and we hold it. I am going to ask the Captain here, if he can let us have two of his cannon and some of his jacktars to man it as gunners. They would be of considerable help if we have to withstand a siege.'

'You have them, sir,' the stern Welsh Captain snapped promptly.

'Thank you, Captain.'

'You will need supplies, too,' the *Diana's* Captain continued. 'Once I have landed your foot, my tars can bring you a longboat full of vittles and whatever extra ammunition you might need. What about water?'

'Beer, you mean,' Sweeney said under his breath and the Captain glared at him.

'There are several fountains in the Golden Pagoda. I have seen them myself,' Bold answered. 'I should hope they will suffice until we are relieved.' He hesitated momentarily, while the others stared at him expectantly. There were scores of things to be done now that the Major had revealed his plan. Why waste further time?

Finally Bold broke his unexpected silence. 'As you know General Campbell is unaware of this new plan of mine. Consequently he will be anticipating that our force has landed on that coast yonder, not at Rangoon. It is expedient, therefore, that he should be informed of the change of plan as soon as possible so that he can come to our relief.'

'And how will that be done, sir?' Sweeney asked a little uneasily.

Bold made no attempt to soften the blow. 'This way. As soon as the *Diana* has landed us and our supplies, it must turn about and find General Campbell's force with all possible speed. They will then change course for Rangoon. . . . ' He let his words trail away, knowing by the looks on their faces that they realized what his decision meant.

It was young Hodgson, however, who put their thoughts into words. Slowly, he said. 'That would mean, sir, that we should be completely cut off, half a thousand miles from our nearest base.'

Bold nodded, watching for any sign of dissent. but there was none, just a look of thoughtful concern as if each man were making his individual decision on the news, coming to terms with it in his own fashion.

'And if General Campbell's force does not reach us in time, sir?' Hodgson pressed home the point.

'But he will, Ensign . . . *he will!*' Bold raised his voice, telling himself that he would not let them dwell on the matter any longer. 'Gentlemen,' he announced with a note of finality in his voice, 'the Captain here informs me we shall be entering the Rangoon delta within the hour. So you have much to do to prepare your men for the assault.' He looked hard at them. 'We attack one hour before dawn. . . . '

THREE: THE BATTLE FOR RANGOON

1

Noiselessly the *Diana*, its engine shut down and powered now by its sail alone, glided down the estuary. The moon had vanished behind the clouds and the only light was that peculiar dirty white glow of false dawn. Still the heavily armed men lining the deck could make out the boats anchored along the numerous jetties and landing places that interrupted the jungle. And by straining their eyes, they could just glimpse the Golden Pagoda, its dome shaped like an inverted speaking-trumpet.

No comment was made. For Bold had ordered the strictest silence. The usual drumroll which summoned the soldiers and sailors to quarters had been forbidden, as had had all external lanterns. Even the horses had been muffled with their feedbags so that they could not give away the *Diana*'s presence.

Each man was landing with three days' cooked provisions, full water-bottles and fifty-six rounds of ammunition, plus his carbine or musket and the usual pack. As Bold surveyed them for the last time, he hoped that none of the long boats would overturn. With the weight of gear the foot were carrying, they'd go straight to the bottom of the river.

He turned to the Ensign, standing along a section of the deck where the rail had been removed, with the hooded horses standing in line swishing their tails and trembling a little with nervousness. 'I have decided the foot will go in first. The horses might cause early alarm. You will follow once you have my signal from the shore.'

'Very good, sir. I shall have a spare horse brought ashore for you.'

'Thank you. But I think I do not feel well enough for riding at the moment, at least for a day or two . . . ' He smiled a little wrily. 'If things go wrong, we can at least eat it.' Hodgson did not reply. He was very fond of his horses. The thought of eating one was repugnant to him. 'All right,' Bold said, 'carry on – and good luck!'

'Good luck to you, too, sir.'

'Thank you, Ensign.'

Hurriedly Bold moved to where the Captain stood supervising the landing operation. To the east the sky was already beginning to lighten. There was no time to lose and both officers knew it. Already a dozen barefoot sailors, their broad-brimmed straw hats flung aside, but with short carbines slung over their brawny shoulders, were beginning to lower the first longboat, two small cannon resting in its centre. The night before the Captain had ordered the pulleys and gears to be well-oiled and the sailors made virtually no noise as they reeled the heavy wooden boat down to the still waters of the delta. Bold nodded his approval and said, 'I shall go with the first boat, Captain. Once we are grounded, we will wade the rest of the way and send her back. If luck's on our side, we'll have the men and the cannon ashore within ten minutes. Once you hear the first sound of firing, please turn about and sail with all dispatch. And thank you for your efforts.'

Solemnly the Welsh Captain, not demonstrative by nature, reached out and placed a hand on Bold's shoulder, 'May God be with you, Major,' he said, 'I shall pray for you this day.'

'Thank you, Captain,' Bold said equally solemnly, though at the back of his mind that cynical little voice told him, 'I always thought God was on the side of the *big* battalions.' He ignored it, and strode over to where the sailors were preparing to lower the first boat carrying Sweeney's men. 'All right,' he said urgently, 'lower away, lads!'

Like grey ghosts, they moved across the smooth surface of the water hardly making a sound, for the sailors had muffled the rowlocks. All was tense expectation and there was none of the usual rough banter among the soldiers. They knew that their very lives depended upon complete

96

surprise and their apprehension was tangible. Bold felt he could smell it on the damp pre-dawn air.

He sensed his own pulse begin to race faster as the bosun up front whispered, 'About a fathom now, sir. We'll be grounding soon.'

Bold nodded his understanding. Awkwardly he drew his sabre. It made a metallic slithering sound as it came out of the scabbard and the solidiers in the packed boat looked at him. They knew what that gesture signified. Next to Bold, Sweeney pulled out his short infantry sword and whispered, 'We'll go through'em like shit through Ma Kelly's goose, sir.' Bold smiled. It was good to have an old soldier like Sweeney at his side in what was to come, even if the fellow's mind was already occupied with the looting ahead.

Minutes later the leading infantrymen were splashing through the shallows, bayonets fixed ready for anything while Sweeney's trumpeter was sounding the signal to the waiting cavalry. With Sweeney and Bold at their head, the infantrymen were doubling down an unpaved street of bamboo houses where yells of alarm and the first ragged volleys of musketfire indicating that Rangoon was waking up to its danger.

Round a corner, a group of Burmese soldiers in conical golden helmets were trying to throw up a makeshift barrier – a handcart, some rickety chairs and a piece of abandoned teak. Some of them stood with their muskets at the ready. 'FIRE!' Sweeney gasped.

His front rank halted and standing erect as if they were back on the range in England, fired as one. The Burmese went down screaming on all sides and Sweeney yelled in triumphant, 'Pick the bones outa that, yer yeller heathens!'

They ran on with Bold slashing to left and right with his sabre at those of the Burmese who still wanted to fight. They sprang over the barrier, bodies littered everywhere. Now Bold could see the Golden Pagoda quite distinctly – it couldn't have been more than two hundred yards away – and already he could hear its huge gongs beating the alarm. 'Hurry up, me lads!' he yelled above the clatter of hooves which indicated Bold's Horse were already ashore too. 'Not far now!'

A half dozen Burmese came skidding down from a side street. They stopped when they saw the redcoats of the foot but there was no time for Sweeney's men to fire. Instead they charged, bayonets levelled. Howling like lunatics they fell upon the Burmese, just as the hidden gunner who had been waiting for them to fall into the trap touched his slow match to the cannon. At that range he couldn't miss. The grape flew everywhere. Burmese and redcoats went down in a confused heap, a gory mess of severed limbs and chunks of red-raw flesh. 'God in heaven,' Sweeney cursed in horror, 'It's like a bloody butcher's in a shambles back home!'

'Get that cannoneer,' Bold commanded and ran forward, sabre at the ready. Then he saw the enemy gunners, hidden down an alley, working frantically to reload their murderous weapon. He gave a great cry of rage and mindless of his own danger, sprang over a mortally wounded redcoat, sprawled in his own blood and gore, and charged the four gunners.

The loader turned to face him, ramrod in his hands and launched a tremendous blow at Bold's head. The Major ducked so that it missed but didn't give the Burmese a second chance. His sabre came whistling down. The Burmese gave a shrill scream and the terribly keen blade split his skull in two.

One of the Burmese lugging the cannonballs dropped his load and reached for his horse pistol. Bold was quicker. His blood-red sabre flashed again. The Burmese went reeling back, staring dumbfounded at the bloody stump where his hand holding the pistol had just been. The other two waited no longer before they fled. And Bold leaned wearily against the glowing cannon, glad that they had done so. For he realized his recent adventure had taken their toll; he wasn't as strong as he should be.

There was no time for rest. The noise from the city was getting ever louder. He could hear the barbaric drumming

98

and beating of gongs which heralded the approach of more Burmese soldiers and the taunting cries of '*lagee . . . lagee*' which he knew meant 'come . . . come' in their language. They had to reach the Golden Pagoda before the main Burmese attack came in; otherwise they would be bogged down in this rabbit-warren of unpaved streets and that would be the end.

'Sweeney,' he cried, running back to the infantry, 'keep 'em moving . . . keep 'em moving!'

'That I will sir,' Sweeney roared back above the snap and crackle of small arms fire, 'like Comeragh buck-rabbits, that I will.'

Despite the tension Bold smiled. Sweeney was playing the real stage Irishman he was, but there was no denying the man's toughness. 'Keep the men roaring like hell, Sweeney. Make all the noise they can. Those yellow devils have got to think that the whole British Army – and the Grand Duke himself personally – are attacking them!'

Howling like men demented, their sword bayonets flashing in the first rays of the rising sun, the little force pushed forward, with the cavalry galloping up to and then in front of them, the troopers waving their sabres wildly, completely carried away by the atavistic madness of battle.

A group of Burmese armed with a kind of pike, which they had hurriedly dug into the earth at their feet to form a rough wall of steel, barred their way. Bold's Horse did not hesitate. With a crazy whooping, they charged. Sabres flashed. Blood spurted in bright-red arcs. The Burmese reeled back, screaming piteously and in an instant the barrier was surmounted and the redcoats advanced again, some of them hanging on to the stirrups of the cavalry. Now the Golden Pagoda was a mere hundred yards or so away. Bold's spirits rose considerably at the sight. His plan was paying off. On the massive steps leading up to the central part of the structure, there were only a half-dozen monks in saffron-coloured robes with razors in their hands. But the razors were not intended for defence, the monks had been using them for the pre-dawn ritual of shaving their heads and eyebrows. So the palace was there to be taken! Yet Bold paused, and turned. To the rear of the column, the tars whom the Captain had lent to him were straining under the weight of two cannon they were towing, as well as the handcart which held their shot and shell. 'Sweeney,' he commanded, 'see that those sailors are given protection. We don't want to lose those—'

The rest of his words were drowned by a tremendous thump, followed an instant later by the smack of a cannon-ball smashing its way into one of the bamboo walls only yards from where he was standing. '*What in the devil's name*,' he began. But once again his speech was interrupted, this time by the wild trumpeting of a crazed elephant. For out of one of the side-streets had emerged an awe-inspiring sight: a massive elephant, its sides padded with shining white armour made of ivory, while from the howdah on its back there emerged a long and ancient cannon – now hectically being reloaded by sweating gunners. Behind the lumbering great beast, there was a mixed force of cavalry and infantry, obviously positioned to guard it against attack. Bold saw the danger immediately. If the elephant could hold them up long enough, then reinforcements could be rushed into the battle and they would never make the Golden Pagoda. 'Ensign,' he roared at the top of his voice above the noise of the mêlée, 'bring down that bloody animal! *At once!*'

By way of response, Hodgson raised himself high in his stirrups, white teeth gleaming against his dark face, and waved his sabre. At full tilt, he and half a dozen of his troopers charged, their horses' hooves skidding and slipping on the cobbles, kicking up showers of angry blue sparks. In a flash all was chaos and confusion. In panic the elephant raised its great head and trumpeted its protest to the morning world, while all around it sabres and bayonets slashed, gouged, hacked, sliced and chopped. A horse went down, its rider screaming shrilly as he was trampled to death under flying hooves. One of Bold's troopers shot over the head of his mount as it suddenly went down onto its forelocks, whinnying in distress, only to land nimbly on his feet like some circus acrobat.

Again the cannon on the howdah fired. Purple flame stabbed the dawn gloom. Even the elephant staggered under the impact of the recoil and great glowing cannon-ball came hurtling straight towards Sweeney's foot, packed and stalled in the narrow street.

'DUCK!' Bold cried desperately, but too late. The ball cut straight through the first file, knocking the redcoats down effortlessly. Suddenly there were dead and dying men lying everywhere on the blood-soaked cobbles.

'Holy Mother of God!' Sweeney yelled, face puce with rage. Before Bold could stop him, he had plunged forward on his own, running straight into the mêlée surging back and forth around the elephant. He raised his pistol and fired at which one of the half-naked gunners threw up his arms wildly and in the next instant pitched forward to his death. Now crazed with rage and excitement, Sweeney started hacking at one of the great animal's back legs with his sword, yelling his head off all the while like a man demented. But Sweeney wasn't mad. Bold could see what he was about. He was trying to force the elephant to run or to fall. Already it was tossing its head from side to side as if plagued by a myriad stinging flies, its red eyes liquid with sudden pain.

One of the Burmese cavalryman brought his scimitar down in a vicious slash. If the blow had landed, it would have sliced Sweeney's skull in two. But Hodgson was quicker. He parried the stroke with a deft flick of his wrist, twisting his opponent's arm. The scimitar tumbled to the cobbles. Hodgson launched a great swing at his opponent. In no time Burmese's yellow face opened up like a split blood-orange, all crimson and oozing gore. Next moment he was swept from his saddle, dead before he hit the ground.

Now the elephant was raising its injured leg, the blood already beginning to seep through the thick grey flesh, feebly trying to kick his assailant away. But Sweeney dodged each kick and then commenced hacking away once more like a dedicated woodman determined to bring down an obstinate tree. By this time Hodgson, too, had seen

101

what Sweeney was about. He joined in, hacking with all his might at the same leg, while at the same time deterring the enemy from closing in on the lone infantryman. Slowly but surely, the elephant was beginning to weaken.

Bold realized he must do something. 'You men in the front rank,' he cried to the stalled infantry, 'fire at the box on that bloody elephant. We've got to stop those gunners firing again. Or we'll all be bloody goners trapped like this!'

The survivors of the last cannoncade needed no urging. Standing or kneeling among their sprawled dead comrades, they aimed at the armoured howdah. Ivory splintered and cracked. Balls howled off into the air. The sweating foot fired, reloaded, biting off the tough end of the cartridge, ramming, reversing, thrusting home the ball and fumbling for the percussion cap to press into the caplock. But slow as their firing was – three rounds per minute – they were keeping the native gunners from manning their piece, while Sweeney and Hodgson, both lathered with sweat now, continued to hack at the obstinate beast.

Suddenly its massive frame started to shake and tremble. The howdah slipped to a crazy angle. Behind their splintered and chipped ivory armour, the gunners hung on for their very lives. The cannon pitched forward. Desperately they tried to hold it. To no avail! It slipped and clattered to the ground. Furiously, scenting victory now, the two officers cut away at the gory red stump, through which the bones gleamed a brilliant white. Although the elephant shrieked, tossing its trunk from side to side with the unbearable pain of it all it somehow it never managed to dislodge them. When it tottered forward, jerking its leg, the two officers showed no mercy, and moved with it. At length the elephant's head sunk. It gave a kind of despairing groan and with a crash slumped to its knees. The strap holding the howdah in place snapped. It came tumbling down and with it the gunners.

Bold waited no longer. 'Forward now, men . . . Forward!'

The cavalry waved their sabres and the foot gave a great cheer. Swearing and laughing they surged, clambering over the grey beast which now lay on its side like a deflated balloon. Gasping for breath, their sword arms red with gore right up to the shoulders, Sweeney and Hodgson joined them.

Here and there shots still rang out, and next to a running Bold a redcoat clasped his hand to his shoulder and said in a matter-of-fact way, 'The yeller buggers have gone an' shot me.' Next moment he keeled over dead. But there was no stopping that charge now. Anyone attempting to do so was bayonetted or sabred down without mercy.

Already they were pelting up the great stairs leading to the interior of the Pagoda, gasping for breath, faces brick-red, eyes wild and unseeing. A group of shaven-headed monks tried to bar their way by linking hands. Bayonets flashed and cruel brassbound musket-butts slammed home. The brothers died on the steps of their own temple.

Bold leaned a little weakly against one of the ornate columns, holding his side, watching his troopers trying to negotiate the steps with their mounts. For he wanted them inside the Pagoda, too. Sweeney came up to him, panting. He had lost his shako and there was a deep cut across the side of his skull. But he was grinning all the same like a Cheshire cat. He raised his bloody sword in mock salute and gasped, 'Well, that got the heathens off'n their yeller arses, sir!'

'That it did,' Bold agreed.

Sweeney let his sight run over the interior chamber greedily. There was gold and ivory everywhere and some of the statues of the Buddha had eyes made of great red rubies. 'Keep me in baccy and doxies for the rest of my born days, sir,' he said and licked his lips greedily. 'Christ, what a place to loot!'

Bold had just opened his mouth to make a suitable reply when he heard it. The sharp blasts of a ship's foghorn. It was the signal he had agreed upon with the *Diana*'s skipper. She was sailing. 'Bugler,' he called above the racket in the great echoing hall, 'sound the victory call. Loud and clear, give it all your strength!'

The bugler, a flaxen-haired youth no more than fourteen, minus his shako and with a rip in his tunic, stepped forward smartly onto the steps and poised himself. He took a deep breath, his rosy cheeks puffed out to their full extent, and blew the call. It echoed over the scene of carnage below, shrill and triumphant, but somehow beautiful. For a moment its call reminded Bold of his long dead father. How he had used to boast of the 'Old Regiment' and how there was nothing more 'beautiful in this world than the sound of bugles at dawn'.

As the boy let his bugle fall, his face suddenly deflated, Bold listened intently for the answering signal. Yes, there it was. One long blast on the *Diana*'s foghorn. Her skipper had understood. They had carried the Golden Pagoda at Rangoon by storm. That would be the news to carry back to General Campbell, wherever he might be at this moment.

For a few seconds, the sound of that blast continued to echo and resound among the low hills which surrounded the Burmese capital. When it was gone altogether, Bold realized that they were now all alone right in the heart of the enemy's capital: a handful of white men and brown men had challenged the whole might of the Lord of the White Elephant and Golden Foot.

2

All that long day they laboured to prepare the Golden Pagoda for the attack to come. Hastily great bales of straw, which the monks had used for their water buffalo, were piled high on top of the steps, with loopholes cut in them for Sweeney's sharpshooters. Behind the straw barricades Bold installed the two naval cannons. In the case of anyone penetrating his first line of defence they would run straight into the tars firing grapeshot.

Already he'd had to stop his infantrymen from raiding the fabulous treasures that surrounded them, and from trying to prize the huge rubies from the largest of the golden Buddhas.

The wells and fountains had proved full and it seemed that there was no way of cutting off their water from outside. Supplies of food were adequate, too at least for a short siege. The men had three days' rations and Hodgson had discovered two water buffalo which had not been driven off by the alarmed Burmese. They would last for several days when slaughtered. The only real problem, as he reported to Bold, was 'Ammunition, sir. The men will have to go very sparingly. Thereafter we'll have to depend upon on what the jolly jack tars brought with them in that little cart.'

Bold frowned. 'I have bad news for you, Ensign,' he retorted. 'Your bloody *jolly jack tars*,' he emphasized the words bitterly, 'went and left their little cart behind when the trouble started. Now then, is there any lead about which we can melt and use to form ball? At least the sailors have plenty of gunpowder.'

Hodgson brightened. 'That's a thought sir. I'll see what the plumbing's like in this place. Let's hope it's made of lead and not gold like the rest of the stuff.'

Thus problem after problem was solved, and in some

haste because Bold would not allow his force to take a rest even at the height of the blistering noon heat. For he reasoned that the Lord of the White Elephant and the Golden Foot would attack very soon.

Yet the Burmese still had not attacked as the long hot day started to draw to a close. Even Bold ordered the troops to stand down for a while to eat, drink and rest. Over the city below them lay an ominous brooding silence, without a single human being in evidence. Even the starving dogs and fat-bellied children had vanished. For all they knew, Rangoon could have been a ghost-town.

Bold knew that was not true. Twice he had caught the glint of glass glistening in the sunlight, as if someone were surveying their positions, and here and there the watchers could glimpse thin streams of grey smoke ascending leisurely into the blue sky to the north of the city. Oh, no, Bold told himself, the Lord of the White Elephant and Golden Foot had not yet deserted his capital.

'What are they up to?' Sweeney asked, as the three officers squatted together in the shade, half-heartedly eating a ration of warm pork and hardtack out of their pannikins. 'Why the devil is his nibs takin' so long to attack? We've been here since dawn after all.'

Bold explained how while he had been a prisoner of the Burmese ruler, he had seen large numbers of enemy soldiers heading north. Perhaps there were no longer sufficient troops present locally for a large-scale attack.

'All the same, sir,' Hodgson had objected, chewing steadily on the rockhard hardtack, 'they wouldn't be so foolish as to leave the capital altogether defenceless. All these eastern potentates are afraid of palace revolutions anyway. This one'd have some troops at hand just to protect himself on that score.'

Bold nodded, head turned to one side now. For he was sure he could hear the sound of hammering and sawing coming from somewhere in the capital. 'You're right, of course, Ensign, and we must take every precaution. But the men are weary and we must not tire them too much.

106

This night, we shall stand three quarters of them down. But at first light everyone stands to.'

'Yessir,' the two junior officers agreed, and finished their unpleasant meal as if grateful to do so.

Sweeney said, 'The longer they put off the attack – whatever his nibs' reasons are – the better.'

'I'm with you there, Sweeney. Every day we gain until General Campbell arrives off that levee is a day won. Now I'll just have a look at the chaps.' He rose and the other two did so as well.

'He's a dandy lad, your major,' Sweeney commented as Bold moved out of earshot. 'Although he's half my age, it is a fine thing to be serving under an officer like that.' He spat on the marble floor of the temple. 'And bad cess on you, my Lord Cavendish.'

The Ensign grinned but said nothing. The ugly old Irishman certainly hated his CO. What a chasm divided Cavendish and Bold. The latter could be harsh, impatient and demanding, but he was always fair. Hodgson wagered to himself that there wasn't a man, brown or white, in the entire ranks of Bold's Horse who wouldn't follow their CO to hell and back.

It was a long night. After the sun set, the darkness seemed to make the brooding tension which hung over Rangoon even greater. Usually at this time, the city would have come to life. Those who had hidden from the sun all afternoon as they did in the East, would come out to gossip and shop. The merchants would be crying their wares. There would be the wail of native music and the night air would be heavy with the pungent spices of the Orient.

This night the only sound was the sawing and hammering which Bold had noted earlier, and which he simply could not fathom. What was going on? Finally some time in the small hours of the morning he drifted off into an uneasy sleep, plagued by strange dreams: three-legged elephants with cannons where their trunks should be; the

107

princess, her legs spread wide, urging him on lasciviously, mouthing obscenities in English. He awoke with a sudden start to find himself tumescent, which annoyed him, for this was not the time for such thoughts. After a moment he realized something else, too. The noises of the previous day had ceased and were replaced by an absolute, total silence. He stumbled to his feet and walked by the weary sentinel, indicating with a touch of his fingers to his lips that the soldier should not stamp to attention. Let his men sleep as long as it was possible to do so.

He stopped at the barricade of hay and then, as an afterthought, clambered on top of it watched by the half-asleep sailors manning the two four-wheeled, wooden cannons. He stood there staring at the silent capital, outlined a stark black in the blood-red ball of the sun which had now appeared on the horizon. His brow puckered in a frown. What was it? Something was different down in the street there. Then he had it. To the left and right two long stockades had appeared, supported by he knew not what. They were made of freshly trimmed teak logs, nailed and bound together and stood some six foot in height. He stared at them in dull incomprehension wondering what the hell they signified. He turned to the bosun in charge of the gunners, 'Did anything happen while I slept?' he asked.

'No sir,' the other replied promptly. 'I snatched a kip till about three bells, sir, and when I had a look over the hay, them log barricades were there. For all I knew the hobgoblins might have brought 'em'.

Bold raised his glass and peered through it at the two new structures. At least they explained the hammering of the previous day. For a while he toyed with the idea of slipping out a troop of his cavalry through the back of the Golden Pagoda, in order to make a reconnaissance of the mystifying structures. Then he decided against it. What if they had been set up as a trap, some form of ambush? The Burmese had a reputation for being a cunning people. He couldn't risk his men. His curiosity would have to remain unsatisfied.

At noon with the sun at its zenith and the waiting soldiers gasping with the heat, their stocks unbuttoned although they had received no order to do so, things began to happen. One of the sentries posted at the hay barricade cried, 'It's moving . . . I swear it is!'

Bold, Sweeney and Hodgson were on their feet in a flash, the sweltering heat forgotten, and as Bold vaulted onto the barricade, he too saw the stockade actually move. For a few moments dozens of bare feet appeared as the big structure was lifted, moved five or ten yards, and then dumped down once more midst tiny clouds of dust. About that time, the gongs started to beat in unmusical Burmese fashion.

Bold made a swift calculation. The left stockade, the closest of the two, was now two hundred yards away from the Golden Pagoda and just within cannon-range of the naval guns. Should he take a chance and fire at it?

'Holy Mary, Mother o' God,' Sweeney cursed, 'that racket's worse than any Kilkenny wake, I do swear. It gets on a man's nerves.'

An undecided Bold had to agree that it did.

Twice more during the passage of the afternoon the sentries reported that the stockades had moved and eventually both of them were within what Hodgson called 'rushing distance' of the pagoda.

Bold had the full garrison under arms. Tension was mounting and he sensed movements he could not see. 'What do you think, Sweeney?' he asked shortly before dusk.

'Cavalry,' Sweeney replied, voice very definite as he peered down below. 'They'll try to rush us first with cavalry. And then whoever's behind them stockades'll come out and attack.'

'So you think the cavalry is just a diversion, Sweeney?'

'Yessir. You saw how difficult it was for your own Horse to get up them steps. They'll come rushing at us, full of piss and vinegar, just like Old Boney's lads trying to make us use up our ammo and rattle us at the same time. Then they'll break to left and right when we've popped off our first volley. The rest'll come at us then on foot. That'll be the way of it.'

The man was an old hand. He was right. That would indeed be the way of it. 'We'll have to go canny with our ammunition, Sweeney.' Bold forced a grin, 'I know that young Ensign of mine has managed to mould some golden bullets for us. But that would be a pretty expensive way of conducting a battle. Let's keep Mr Hodgson's golden shot for an emergency.'

Sweeney's eyes glistened. 'Ay, ye're right there, sir. Them bullets is loot, not to be wasted on yellar heathens.'

The clamour of gongs had reached fever pitch. Drums had joined in to build an incessant throbbing which started to get on the nerves of the men. Their NCOs had to go among them, calming them, telling them to 'get that finger off'n yet trigger, Jones 75 or you'll be in trouble . . . ' and, 'watch yersen, Hawkins 703. Pay no heed to them drums. They'll be playing their penny-whistles next and bringing out the bloody brown bear for a dance.' Bold shook his head in admiration. British NCOs, where did they breed men like these: unrattled, imperturbable and calm as as if they had gone through this sort of thing dozens of times before.

As if some invisible conductor had given the signal, the cacophony ceased. In the new silence, officers half-raised their swords, as if to give the signal to fire. Bold stared wide-eyed. And then it started.

Abruptly from the left stockade, a mob of horsemen erupted, jostling and pushing at each other, as they urged their mounts into a gallop. Even so, Bold was absolutely calm. 'Stand your men by, Lieutenant Sweeney. Don't let them start till I give the command.'

Closer and closer the cavalry came, filling the street from one side to the other. Now Bold could see them quite clearly: yellow men with the usual conical helmets on their shaven skulls, a small brass shield protecting their left sides, some of them holding the reins of their flying mounts in their mouths so that they had the freedom of both hands. He couldn't help nodding his approval in a professional manner. He had fought both white and native cavalry. These were veterans all right. Bold let them come, while all around him the NCOs were hissing, 'Steady now . . . wait for it, lads . . . steady!' He knew the men wanted the relief of being able to loose off a volley at the riders. In a minute or more they'd be at the hay barricade. Bold hesitated no longer. He raised his sabre and cried. '*Now*!'

Sweeney bellowed above the hollow clatter of the many hooves, 'Let 'em have it, lads!'

Like oversized marbles, the round stones gilded with gold leaf – which Sweeney's men had chipped from the frieze that ran round the central area of the temple – went tumbling and bouncing down the steps right into the first wave of riders. They had an immediate effect. Horses went down on all sides.

'One volley now;' Bold yelled into the chaos.

'Fire!' Sweeney cried gladly.

From behind their firing holes, the infantry struck the second wave of riders below the steps with a tremendous volley of concentrated lead. The salvo stopped them completely in their tracks. But Bold had no time to observe the result of the second wave. There were a good dozen or more of the cavalry on their feet on the steps. 'Ensign!'

'Sir!'

'Over the top now! Slaughter them. No quarter. They have to be taught a lesson.'

'Sir!'

'And bring back as much ammunition as you can. Go!'

Hodgson swung himself effortlessly over the barricade. Next minute, not even waiting to see if the score of men specially selected for this task were following him, he was clattering down the steps, slashing the air with his sabre as he ran.

What followed was not war; it was slaughter. The shocked Burmese, still trying to extricate themselves from their dead, injured and crazed mounts, had no chance. The troopers ran amok. Whooping and yelling crazily, they slashed and cut, hewing down an enemy who seemed

111

to accept death like sheep led to slaughter. Within minutes the Burmese were sprawled among their dead horses, with only one lone survivor on his knees, holding his hands above his head in the classic pose of supplication, asking for mercy. But no mercy was being given this day. A sabre hissed down remorsely. He keeled over, his skull cleaved in two and peeling apart like a neatly dissected coconut.

A moment or two later the troopers were grabbing whatever weapons and ammunition they could, pelting back to their own positions, grinning and yelling in triumph at their achievement. Bold helped a sweating Hodgson over the pile of hay and relieved him of the pouch of bullets he was carrying. 'Good work, Ensign,' he said, 'you certainly put a stop to them.'

'Thank you, sir. The men did well.'

Bold noted the lack of elation in the young officer's voice and there was no smile of triumph on his sweat-lathered face. 'Anything wrong?' he snapped, as Hodgson dropped behind the barrier.

'No sir, not really,' the other men answered, lowering the two muskets he had seized with a sigh of relief. 'But this is just *one* day. How many more can we survive, if the *Diana* doesn't come soon?'

To that overwhelming question, John Bold had no answer.

3

By dawn the following day the two barricades of teak logs had moved right to the bottom of the great steps, where the dead bodies had already begun to bloat, with great clouds of blue flies hovering above them. A hundred or so yards back, two new barricades had also appeared and the Burmese positions were full of noise and commotion. Columns of blue smoke drifted upwards in the still morning air and the watchers up above could glimpse occasional movement in the dark shadows that lay between the bamboo houses.

One hour later the bombardment started. From behind the second line of barricades mortars boomed, followed by great whirling cannisters of explosive which detonated on impact to send first-sized chunks of red hot metal howling in every direction.

The mortar bombs were not the only danger. As if by magic, firing slots had appeared in the first two stockades, through which the sharpshooters aimed their weapons, targeting anyone who exposed himself. Twice Bold, trying to assess the situation below, had near misses when balls howled off the marble close to his head and showered him with splinters. But the increasing fire, which by midday was causing several casualties, was not Bold's main problem. Most of his men, foot and horse, were veterans and knew how to look after themselves in a bombardment. His main poser was to decide where the enemy might attack next. For it was clear the build-up in their numbers below indicated they were preparing to assault the Golden Pagoda, once again. His own numbers were naturally limited and as he expressed it to a sweating Sweeney, who had taken to wearing a gilded washing bowl on his shaven head whenever he was close to the firing, 'We can't be everywhere at one and the same time, Lieutenant. If they make a feint to our front for instance, but push in their main attack to the rear, they'll catch us off-guard and outnumbered.'

Sweeney agreed and added, 'Major, I have posted a man up there,' he indicated the roof of the pagoda, 'where yon gallery runs around the cup —'

'Cupola,' Bold supplied the word for him.

'Ay, that's it. Thank you, sir. Well I've got a man up there, poor fellah, it must be devilish hot. But he'll give us ample warning of any attack.'

'Perhaps,' Bold said unconvinced. 'For all we know though, Sweeney, when they do attack they'll bring him under such fire that he'll be forced to hide behind the balustrade before he can alert us.'

'Aach, them yeller heathens couldn't hit old Riley's barn door at fifty —' Sweeney's confident boast ended with a yelp of pain, as a ball smashed into the pillar just above his head and showered him with sharp fragments of marble.

The day progressed in constant alarm and uncertainty, with most men praying for darkness so that they would at least be liberated from the fire of the sharpshooters. But even as dusk came, it brought no relief. By means of firebombs shot at the Pagoda by mortars, the whole front of the temple was made as light as day and the dreaded snipers could continue their evil work. As Sweeney complained to Bold, 'Why my poor lads cannot even pull their britches down for a crap in peace, Major! Them damned sharpshooters aim straight for the arse!'

At ten that night, with most of the troops unable to sleep due to the noise, a rocket roared and burst into an arc of twinkling silver stars above the cupola. All eyes flashed upwards in wonder, whilst from his station up there the lone sentry cupped his hands and yelled urgently, 'Gentlemen, down there, they're forming up behind the second line of barricades. Hundreds of 'em. I can—' He shrieked before tumbling over the parapet, hitting the marble floor below to lay like a crumped sack.

Ashen with fear and shock, Bold turned to the bugler

114

'Sound the call to quarters,' he snapped brutally, 'Come on, lad, let's be having you!' But the men defending the barricade heeded no trumpet call to make them spring into action. Already they'd fixed their sword-bayonets, waiting for their NCOs to allow them to fire. For below, outlined by the red flames of the firebombs, the first barricades were moving step by step up the stairs. Bold could not help thinking, it was like something out of one of the terrifying Germanic fairy tales his mother had read to him as a child. 'Fire at will,' he cried above the tramping of feet and the rattle of native gongs, 'Aim at their legs. . . . FIRE!'

A ragged crackle of fire erupted the length of the barrier. Timber splintered and vomited flame. Here and there a Burmese shrieked and slammed to the blood-stained steps. But still that strange wall of wood continued moving forward. There was something awesome and inevitable about it. Bold watched as if hypnotized. It was only when Sweeney yelled, 'Sir, we've got to do something soon or they'll be through our defences in a minute . . . and the other lot's forming up for the charge below,' that he re-awoke to the imminent danger. There was nothing for it but to play his last card.

He cupped his hands above his lips so he could be heard and cried, 'Pull the hay to one side, you men . . . and then retire ten paces!'

'What—' Sweeney began to protest, but Bold was not listening to him. Instead he cried at the uneasy naval gunners, 'Get those cannon in position. When I give the order, fire shot . . . Now get on with it. Quick!'

While the infantry ripped at the bales of hay to clear the way, the gunners busied themselves with their four-wheel cannon. All the time Bold fumed with impatience, as the barricade came closer and closer and the Burmese fired ever more rockets – colouring the night sky a vivid scarlet. He told himself that the end of the world might well look like this.

'The barrier's down, sir,' a red-faced NCO yelled from

the hay in the same instant that the bosun in charge of the guns cried, 'Ready to fire, now, sir.'

Standing some five yards behind Bold, Ensign Hodgson raised his sabre. Behind him the twenty men who had slaughtered the enemy cavalry earlier, gripped their weapons more tightly. They knew what the Ensign was going to do. Without waiting for instructions or orders from Major Bold, he would rush the stockade once the gunners commenced firing. And this time they were not going to escape unscathed. There were simply too many of the Burmese. Down below hundreds of enemy soldiers jostled for position, crying and shouting in their own language, obviously high on bhang and waiting for the order to charge. Bold could wait no longer; he shouted at the top of his voice, 'FIRE!'

The two cannons exploded simultaneously. Dense smoke erupted from their muzzles as they bucked on their wheels, running back with the recoil, as far as their ropes would allow. At that range the gunners couldn't miss. The solid shot struck the teak wall right in its centre. It gave an audible shudder. Splintered timber rained through the air and dropped to the ground screaming. Sweating and cursing, the naval guncrew sponged, loaded and rammed with incredible speed. 'FIRE!' Bold yelled, sensing that their attackers were weakening, for the timber wall had stopped moving.

Again the two cannons thundered and even as they did so, Bold commanded the sweating gunners, 'Now load with cannister – *at the double!*'

Down below the enemy stockade trembled and quivered like a live thing as two cannonballs slammed into its centre once again, ripping great holes in the timber upon impact. Suddenly Bold's heart leapt with joy. The wall of wood was slipping.

It was a gunners' dream. They didn't even wait for Bold's order, but fired the cannister straight into the Burmese. They hadn't a chance. The deadly shells exploded right in their midst, turning the steps into a charnel house within seconds. Now it was the Ensign's turn. 'At them, lads!' he cried in English, waving his sabre furiously, and even though most of his troopers did not understand English, they understood the intention.

Screaming and cursing, carried away by the unreasoning excitement of combat, they streamed forward, slaughtering the handful of survivors without mercy. Within minutes it was all over and by the time Hodgson's men had begun to ascend the blood-covered steps once more, Bold knew he had survived another day. Suddenly he felt as if someone had opened a tap and all energy had drained from his lean body.

John Bold was not going to be allowed to rest just yet. From below there came another burst of native music. Bold groaned and next to him a hatless Sweeney cursed, 'Won't the bluidy yellow heathens allow a poor Christian man a wee bit o' rest? Are the buggers gonna cannonade us agen?' But the sounds did not herald a fresh outburst of firing. Instead a procession of six Burmese carrying flaming naphtha torches appeared, lighting the way for an obviously important personage. In their centre one figure carried a golden umbrella, which Bold knew indicated high rank from his visit to the court of the Lord of the White Elephant.

Sweeney licked his lips. 'It would be worth using one of Ensign Hodgson's golden ball on yon wee feller,' he said, a nasty look in his bloodshot eyes. 'Even me, I couldn't miss him at that range.'

Bold shook his head. 'No, I don't know what the feller's up to, but it's obvious he's not out to do us any harm. Let's wait and see what he's about.'

At the bottom of the steps, the procession halted. The torch-bearers, on command, held their torches even higher so as to illuminate the man with the golden umbrella. Now the latter advanced, dangling his umbrella over his shoulder so that his face could be seen clearly under the conical helmet.

Bold gasped. It was none other than his interpreter during his stay in the golden cage. It was Po!

Po smiled politely and called up, 'I can see you, Major Bold. May I speak with you?'

'Jesus, Mary and Joseph,' Sweeney exclaimed, 'yon wee heathen speaks English like what we do – and he knows yer name, Major!'

Bold ignored him and called, 'What do you want to speak of, Po?'

'Your surrender.'

'Surrender – *never*!' Bold cried angrily.

Po remained smiling. 'Let me tell you something, Major Bold. Our fisher-folk report that General Campbell's fleet has been becalmed off the Andaman Isles for the last week. Soon our great armies to the north will commence their march on the Arracan under Mala Bandoola.'

'So?' Bold said defiantly, though his spirit was sinking at the news of General Campbell's predicament.

'So, you achieve no purpose by continuing your defence of the Golden Pagoda, and the Lord of the White Elephant and Golden Foot's offer still holds good. My lord still needs a guide for the route to Calcutta.' Po allowed himself a little laugh. 'Although now you are here and General Campbell is becalmed in the middle of the Bay of Bengal, I suspect our army will have little problem in conquering your city.'

John Bold was tempted to yell something obscene, but he restrained himself. After all the fate of his men depended upon his judgement. He asked, 'And if we do not accept your offer?'

'You say not "I" but "we". That is exact. You will be shown no mercy. All of you will be killed with no exceptions, even you Major John Bold will die.'

'Ay, that might be, you yeller bugger,' Sweeney growled at Bold's side, 'but ye've got to catch us first.' He hawked fiercely and spat over the hay bale, as if in contempt.

Bold did not respond at once. Without the relief that Campbell would bring, he doubted if he could hold the Golden Pagoda much more than two more days, especially if the Burmese continued their attacks. His forces were using up their supplies rapidly, especially of ammunition, and once they had lost their superior fire power, reduced to sword and bayonet it would be a matter of man against man. In this the Burmese outnumbered them ten to one. Should he trust Po and surrender to save the men's lives? It was a decision he could not make there and then. He needed to parley. Thus it was to the astonishment of Sweeney, Hodgson and the other officers that John Bold said, 'Po, I cannot decide just like that,' he snapped his fingers. I need time to consider . . . *please*.'

That 'please' had the desired effect. Po obviously believed Bold was weakening. So he agreed, 'You shall have until dawn to make your decision, my dear Major Bold. As a token of our good faith, we shall now cease all aggressive action. There will be no more firing on your positions. But hear this, please. If you do not comply with our wishes on the morrow to disarm and accept the protection of my master, then we shall show no mercy. Not one of you will live.'

'Ach,' Sweeney snarled, 'tell yon man, sir to go and crap in his cap!'

Bold did nothing of the sort. Instead, he said in a voice which was without any emotion, 'I understand, Po. Good night.'

The little Burmese bowed, 'I return in the morning.'

The men bearing the flaming torches set off at a solemn pace. Five minutes later they had disappeared within their own lines and a great silence fell over the battlefield. It was as if the enemy positions had gone to sleep.

'Confident buggers, aren't they?' Sweeney commented, searching Bold's unshaven features for some sign as to the way he was thinking now. 'A couple of fresh companies from the good old Forty-First Foot and we'd make the buggers run!'

Bold nodded a little sadly. 'You might be right, Sweeney,' he said. 'Unfortunately the good old Forty-First is five hundred miles away from here this night. Now leave me to think.'

119

4

General Campbell was feverish and angry. It was not just his old malaria, caught all those years before in the Pennisula, flaring up again; it was the news that the Welsh Captain of the *Diana* had brought. Hadn't it also been a damned bible-thumping Welshman who'd brought the order for them to start that disastrous retreat of the British Army back in the old war? The Welsh were a nation, he concluded, which should be permanently barred from the affairs of England. He stared at the naval Captain. 'Well, I am glad that Major Bold is alive,' he commenced, feeling his cheeks flush with the fever. 'I am glad, too, that he made his own decisions and captured yon Golden Pagoda place. If this is so then he's in a position to dominate the enemy's capital,' he finished. 'However, what I don't like about Major Bold's situation is that because we're becalmed off these damned islands, twiddling our thumbs waiting for the damned wind to come, we can't go to his aid.

'Sir, if I may make a suggestion,' the Captain said, 'As soon as I saw that the fleet was at anchor and becalmed, I realized there could only be one way to transport troops to Rangoon to the rescue of Major Bold and his command.'

'Well, get on with it, man!'

'I could sail the *Diana* back with as many as I could cram in in the holds. I could lighten my load of coal in the hope that there would be plenty of wood to be found for fuel in Burma, and use the empty bunkers for men . . . ' His voice trailed away, for he could see the General was no longer listening. 'What is it, sir?'

Campbell did not feel like explaining, but did so. 'I know not what yon ship o' yourn, the *Diana* could hold in the way of men even with its coal bunkers emptied,

120

but I doubt if it could be more than a company – and a company, I am afraid, would be a mere drop in the ocean.'

'But sir,' the Welshman persisted, 'my plan is more than just the *Diana*. I am sure that we could get up enough power not only to transport a company of foot in the *Diana*, but also to tow a laden trooper.'

Campbell forgot his fever and his throbbing headache. 'Say that again, Captain!' he exclaimed.

The Welshman elaborated and Campbell roared, '*Capital*! Why in that way, we could take Cavendish's regiment and perhaps half a battalion of native infantry – a thousand men or more. That should do the job.' He raised his voice. 'Did you hear that Colonel Cavendish?' he yelled.

Ever since his company had disappeared on General Campbell's orders, Cavendish had affected aristocratic disdain in that officer's presence. In his heart he still burned with rage and longed to be able to return to Calcutta where he could report the former's scandulous behaviour to his uncle. Indeed, he was secretly pleased that the invasion fleet was becalmed. It might mean the failure of the whole expedition. That, with what he had to report to his uncle, would mean the ruination of 'Highland Archie'. Now he frowned as Campbell repeated the news. This development could mean the failure of his plans, damn the fellow! 'Do you think it wise, General?' he queried. 'I well remember the Great Duke,' he meant the Duke of Wellington, 'telling my father that he would have lost Waterloo if he had divided his army into penny packets of tea as his advisers recommended. Aren't we doing the same – I mean if we split up our force, making it easier for the enemy to beat them bit by bit?'

Campbell thought of the time when he had seen the Duke, though he hadn't had that title then, squatting in a ditch by the side of a Spanish road with his britches down, suffering from the same thin shits that had afflicted them all in that country. But he didn't tell Cavendish that. Instead he said, 'It is the only way, Colonel. I can't leave Bold to be slaughtered in Rangoon.'

Cavendish didn't care who Bold was and what he was

doing in Rangoon. All he was concerned with was the disgrace of General Campbell. 'Well, sir, you are the commander of this force,' he said, louder than usual, so that everyone would be able to hear his views and mark them for later, 'and I must obey loyally. However may I be allowed to register my protest?'

'Register away, Colonel,' Campbell said heartily, his mind buzzing with plans now, the malaria totally forgotten. What did he care what the fool thought!

'I think it is a highly dangerous and foolhardy thing to do so, sir. Six thousand of us together can surely beat those yellow heathens.' He shrugged, 'One thousand – I have my doubts.'

'Then have your doubts, Colonel Cavendish,' Campbell said quite calmly. He knew exactly why Cavendish had spoken to him in this manner in front of the other officers assembled on the deck. It was an old trick of letting others fall into the privy while you came out smelling of attar of roses. 'Now I expect you to collect your battalion and make arrangements for sailing.' He turned to the Welshman. 'When can you sail, Captain?' he snapped.

'On the hour, sir.'

'Good. Did you hear, Cavendish?' there was irony in the General's voice now, 'We sail on Rangoon on the hour.'

Five hundred miles to the east, John Bold spent the night with little sleep. Rangoon was uppermost in his mind, too. He knew Po and his master were desperate to have an end to the siege. With the Golden Pagoda in enemy hands, Rangoon was in constant danger. But somehow John Bold doubted they would honour their promise to spare the defenders. Although he knew little of their religion, he realized that merely in being armed within the pagoda, they had committed sacrilege. Would the common people of the country let this pass? He felt not. The Burmese themselves had actually fired at the Golden Pagoda and had shed blood on the steps leading up to it, but so far had not spilled blood inside the temple itself. Would not an *inside* attack be regarded by the pious Burmese as sacrilege and, if so, could the Lord of the White Elephant really make his troops storm into the pagoda? In other words, was Po trying to *bluff* him into surrender? It was an intriguing thought.

Still worrying at the problem, Bold finally fell asleep, but not for long. Someone was tugging at his sleeve, whispering in order not to wake the others, 'Sir . . . sir.'

'What is it?' He opened his eyes, blinked and focused on the wizened face of Riding Master Jones. Each night Jones and a handful of the most experienced troopers carried out patrols to the rear of the Golden Pagoda where the forest started. It was highly dangerous work because the trees cut down visibility to a dozen yards or so. But highly necessary because Bold knew the forest could easily have hidden a whole army. Now he woke fearing just that. 'What is it, Jones?' he repeated urgently. 'Bad news?'

'Well, sir, there's a queer old stink started up back there. Not yer usual blackie stink, different somehow. Never smelled nothing like it before. And then there's this, sir.' Jones clicked his fingers like a conjuror about to produce a white rabbit. The *rissaldar* appeared from the gloom, guiding a small and completely swathed figure before him.

'A prisoner?' Bold demanded. Jones chuckled, 'In a way, if you like, sir. But ye don't often see prisoners like this one. *Rissaldar*!'

The cloth which covered the 'prisoner's' face was tugged back and John Bold gasped with surprise. 'Why . . . why it's her!' he stuttered amazed.

'Yes, it is I, John,' the princess said gravely in English to his even further amazement.

Hurriedly he rose to his feet and commanded, 'All right, Jones and you, *Rissaldar*. You can get back to your duties now. You have done well.' He waited till they had gone and then turned back to the girl, who was now gazing up at him with her beautiful dark face. 'Well?' he queried.

'John, I came to warn you,' she said urgently. 'It was

not easy smuggling myself through the forest, but I knew I had to.'

'But why? I am your country's enemy.'

'Because when you escaped,' her eyes suddenly filled with tears, 'they killed my father. He was no friend of the Lord of the White Elephant and he was their hostage, too.' She dabbed her eyes, 'I was at fault for letting you go – so they killed him.'

Bold cursed softly and felt suddenly shamed. Of course, someone would have had to suffer for his escape. He had always hoped it might be the servants. 'I am very sorry, princess.'

She pressed his arm softly and he could feel the electric warmth of her flesh. 'Besides,' she whispered, lowering her gaze, 'I love you, John Bold.'

The words were spoken plainly, without artifice; they were the simple expression of a truth that Bold realized he had received from no woman before.

Gently he took her hand and guided her to his blanket. 'Come, sit down here,' he whispered, 'and tell me everything.' She did so in a low voice with the men snoring all around her. She related how her father, a progressive aristocrat, had sent her to Calcutta for her schooling, something which had gained him an enemy in the old-fashioned Lord of the White Elephant. For apparently there had been traditionally much rivalry among Burma's élite for possession of the throne, with new cliques being formed all the time. Her father and the progressives had been banished while she had been in India. But she herself had been received at court, because the Lord of the White Elephant wanted to marry her off safely to one of his own supporters. When John Bold had been captured, she had been assigned to be his companion – and watchdog. At the same time her father had been brought out of exile to be used as a hostage for her loyalty and efficiency.

While she talked, Bold's nostrils were constantly assailed by the strange smell which Jones had mentioned and like the NCO he was unable to identify it. It didn't worry him. He had been in the subcontinent for ten years now; he was used to its strange ways. When she told him that the Lord of the White Elephant had vetoed an armed attack on the interior of the Golden Pagoda, Bold nodded his understanding. His reasoning about sacrilege had been right. Then he reminded her that she'd come with a warning.

She nodded urgently. 'Yes, my dear John. Can you not smell that odour? In our tongue we call it "the fat that comes from the earth"*, she explained. 'The country people use it mixed with sand – for it is very dangerous on its own – to cook their food. They stir it well into a pile of sand and then ignite it. It burns thus for a long time. Otherwise, without the sand, it would explode into violent fire. And all this long night, Po's people have been preparing it in large quantities – just in the forest to your rear. And . . . if you refuse to surrender on the morrow, he will ignite that fat. I have seen such things happen before by accident. There will be a tremendous fire.' She looked very afraid, as if she had just realised the full import of her words.

'You mean if Po and his master can't make us surrender and can't attack us with armed force, they will burn us out? That way they will incur no sacrilege.' She nodded numbly and John Bold was stumped. If he didn't surrender on the morrow to Po, he and his men would be burned alive in the Golden Pagoda – or forced out into the open by the flames and shot down mercilessly by Po's sharpshooters. What was his next move?

---

* The princess, of course, refers to Burma's as yet undiscovered oil fields around Rangoon. Over one hundred years later when the British were forced to abandon Rangoon by the attacking Japanese and set light to those same wells, they burned for a solid six months in 1942.

5

Anxiously General Campbell eyed the horizon to the east. Ahead the *Diana* puffed and churned, using full power to tow the big three-deck trooper, crammed with nearly 1,500 men and their equipment. For a day now everything had been going well, but as he watched the sky Campbell realized they were in for a storm. Already the trooper's limp sails were beginning to billow out intermittently. The sky was leaden and lowering, the air heavy. As for the damp heat it was monstrous, making every slight movement an effort.

The question was, Campbell told himself, whether the storm would be to their advantage. A head wind would do them no good. Indeed it might even part the cable between them and the *Diana* and leave them wallowing in the troughs – the barefoot tars perched aloft, fighting madly to keep the sails from being ripped to shreds. 'Damnit!' he cursed. 'Must everything be against us?'

Down, below squatting on his bunk in the heavy cabin, Cavendish sipped Portuguese brandy and listened to the sounds of the impending storm. In a way he was half-afraid, the cabin lamp was beginning to swing to and fro at an alarming rate, but at the same time he was pleased. Anything which might sabotage the success of Campbell's expedition gave him delight. So he raised his glass in mock toast. 'Blow, winds, . . . blow!' he began, then forgot the rest of the quotation. So he laughed, 'Blow like hell . . . and send the lot of us all the way back to Calcutta!' He drained his brandy and then flung his glass against the wall.

Five minutes later the heavens opened up. The little steam ship *Diana* gamely fought the waves, riding up and down in great troughs of water. While on the bridge of the trooper, Campbell clung on for dear life, fighting back nausea and, watching the cable between the two ships grimly. Sometimes it slackened, only to tighten moments later with a violent vibrating as if it might split at any moment. At his side, the master of the trooper shook his head time and time again, as if they could only expect the worse, now. Finally Campbell bellowed at him, the words snatched from his mouth by the howling wind, 'Will ye nair look like a bluidy frightened virgin the first time she sees a male tool!'

'But, General,' the other man roared back, 'we can't go on much longer like this! The masts'll go. There's only one thing for it, sir. Cut the cable, rig full sail and run with the wind.'

'But the wind is coming from the east,' Campbell objected, raindrops lashing his face, 'that'd mean we'd have to sail back the way we've come.'

The master only nodded. As if to prove his words, that same instant the wind gave the trooper a tremendous buffet. There was the sound of a sail ripping and an ominous creaking noise from the main mast.

Campbell had no choice. 'All right, then,' he roared. 'Have it yer own damned way! Strike the bloody cable, if you have to!' With that he turned his back on the Captain, as if he could not bear to look at him any longer.

Five minutes later the job was done and the lightened *Diana* was ploughing on through the great swell alone. Within the hour, she had vanished over the horizon, leaving the trooper to run before the storm the way she had come, her sails unfurled. Down in his swaying cabin, Cavendish smiled happily. He had already guessed what was happening. Now despite his increasing nausea, he had a warm feeling of triumph. The Campbell expedition was a failure and the man who had led it doomed to disgrace.

Whatever General Campbell thought, the skipper of the *Diana* was a conscientious and determined man. It was now nearly a week since he had landed the Bold force at Rangoon and signalled his departure on the ship's foghorn, and he could well imagine the parlous state the group of soldiers and sailors might now find themselves in. With the whole might of the Burmese nation ranged against them, they would need every little bit of help and he was determined to give them all the assistance he could. He reasoned that the appearance of the *Diana* in the Rangoon delta might just swing the balance in Bold's favour. The Burmese might think the steam ship heralded the approach of the main invasion fleet. A show of strength plus a cannonade from his remaining guns might do the trick. But the essential thing was to arrive there in time. He stared down at the open hold where the lascars toiled to feed the boilers, and cried through his speaking trumpet, 'Move, men . . . MOVE!' He had commenced a race with time.

In the Golden Pagoda the air was now so scented by the 'fat that comes out of the earth', that some of the soldiers had taken to wearing dirty rags around their lower face to keep out the stench. For a while Bold had toyed with the idea of getting his men to dig a wide ditch to the rear of the pagoda, over which any fire would be unable to spring. But just before dawn a fresh wind from the east had sprung up and made that idea impractical. The wind would only carry the fire across. Then he had mulled over the thought of attempting a mass breakout to penetrate the Burmese lines and escaping into the forest. He knew his troopers, mounted as they were, would probably get through. But what about the foot? They would be burdened with their wounded comrades, too, and they'd stand little chance of surviving.

In the end it was Sweeney who'd come up with the only idea to offer some hope. It was to kill Po and therefore deprive the other side of their interpreter. For with Po out of the action, there'd only be the princess who could speak both English and the native tongue. And Sweeney had seen the way she looked at John Bold.

'But what good would that do, Sweeney?' Bold voiced his first reaction. 'They'd take it that we don't want to surrender and then they'd put their devilish plan into operation.'

Sweeney winked and then gave Bold what he obviously thought was a very cunning look. 'Only if they thought the shot that killed yon yeller fellah came from us. What if it didn't come from the pagoda, but from their own lines? We could sneak one of our shooters over there. They might take it to be an accident. Ye know what them heathen buggers are like with firearms. It'd give us more time till they found out at least.'

Bold could see what Sweeney was about, of course. He knew that the assassination of Po, no bad thing in itself, could delay the end by a day, perhaps hours. And gaining time was of the essence. Why should he believe Po that the British invasion fleet was becalmed off the islands? Perhaps it was only one of his tricks. For all he knew the fleet was already turning into the delta to relieve him. If not though, the plan was hopeless as a long-term solution. Short-term, however, it had its merits.

'All right, Sweeney,' he said finally. 'Let us say I accept your plan, who can I expect to risk his neck in a business like this? You know the chances of coming out of it, not smelling of shit, are virtually nil.'

Sweeney grinned back at him like the cocky little Irish countryboy he had been before he'd accepted the King's Shilling. 'Who d'ye think, yer honour?' he said, the old brogue all too obvious now, 'No other than Brigit Sweeney's handsome son.'

Five minutes later Sweeney was ready. He had rid himself of his regimentals and was clad in nondescript native clothes, taken from one of the dead still littering the steps. He'd smeared his face with dirt and for weapons he carried a native knife thrust in the sash around his waist and one of the Dutch repeater carbines, also taken from the Burmese slain.

Bold frowned as Hodgson wound a native turban expertly around Sweeney's head and said, 'Have you thought of those rubies, Sweeney, the baccy and the doxies they'll buy?'

Sweeney grinned, 'Ach, sir,' he said, 'I never did think I'd get back home in the first place, and even if I did, I knew I'd die as poor as when I started. Better, if God wills it, to die as a man, with yer bloody head up than to snuff it as a dribbling dotard in the poorhouse.' His grin broadened. 'Now wasn't that a speech and a half for a poor bog Irishman?' He straightened up and stuck out his big hand. 'Wish me luck, sir?'

Bold thrust out his own hand and they shook. Then Sweeney was off, sticking to the shadows, moving with surprising speed for a man of his age. Minutes later he had vanished from view and there was nothing the defenders could do save wait and pray.

Only when the drums and the gongs began to sound half an hour later, did Bold wake from his gloomy reverie. Hodgson was at his side, waiting for orders. The infantry had already stood to, automatically. Now Bold turned and snapped, 'All right, Ensign, saddle up and have your troopers standing by for action.'

'Sir!' The Ensign doubled away swiftly, glad that the tension was broken at last. Now, he told himself as he ran to where Riding Master Jones was already cursing the men to their feet, the events of the next hour or so would decide all their fates. The die was about to be cast.

Ten minutes thereafter the cavalry had saddled up and the troopers were holding the heads of their nervous mounts, when the same little procession as before emerged from the enemy positions below. This time Po was not attended by torch bearers; instead his companions and servants bore a silk canopy to protect him from the rays of the rising sun, even though Po himself still carried the golden umbrella which was the symbol of his rank. A vain man after all, Bold told himself, as he watched the approach.

He let his gaze wander. There was quite a crowd of natives now standing at the barricades and he wondered if Sweeney was with them. They were all armed in one way or another, so one more armed man wouldn't stand out among them. Or was he concealed in some of the trees

130

standing to left and right of the street? They would offer the best possible form of concealment and give Sweeney the best chance of slipping away after the assassination. But at the back of his head, a familiar cynical voice sneered, 'Do you really think Sweeney's got a snowball's chance in hell? Once those heathens have discovered what direction the shot has come from, they'll not leave a stone unturned until they find the culprit. Your Irishman is a dead man already!' And John felt the little voice inside his skull was right.

Po halted at the foot of the stairs and removed the silken handkerchief from his nose with which he had been keeping out the stench of the dead. He looked upwards and the princess, who had now rejoined Bold, shrank back into the shadows as he did so. She feared being seen by the little man.

They exchanged greetings and Po announced, 'You have had all night to consider the kind offer of my master the Lord of the White Elephant, Major.'

Bold tried to form his answer slowly, all the while playing for time and listening to the voice in his head that repeated, *'Where is Sweeney . . . where is the damned man?'*

' . . . now Major, how say you—'

The crack, like tinder-dry wood being snapped under foot at the height of the summer, surprised even Bold when it came. He gave a little start. As for Po, he faltered and a puzzled look appeared on his face. He coughed as a sudden surge of blood came from the side of his mouth and began to dribble down his chin. His knees started to give. The golden umbrella tumbled and only a moment later he pitched forward to lay in the white dust, quite dead.

6

Sweeney was running for his life. He had thrown away
the carbine as soon as they had spotted him in the tree,
immediately after the panic had commenced. Now he was
dodging in and out of the little bamboo houses, frantically
trying to find some means of escape. There were about
six of them after him, faces suffused with rage, waving
their weapons angrily. He doubled down yet another mean
street, children suddenly crying at the sight of him, dogs
barking and snapping at his flying heels.

Sweeney had been brought up in the tradition that one
Irishman was worth more than any ten foreigners and he
still felt that if he turned and confronted his pursuers, he
could deal with them armed only with his short infantry
sword. But then, he reasoned, the rest of the mob would
be attracted and that would be that. To his front he saw
one of the typical water courses of that part of Rangoon.
A scum-covered narrow stretch of water that fed into the
delta. To the right of it there were a few bamboo houses
– built on stilts to avoid the annual flooding.

Sweeney flung a desperate look behind him. They were
about fifty yards off. He dived forward and hit the water
with a splash, then he was swimming all-out using the
awkward paddle he had learned as a boy in the ponds of
his native Sligo. Behind him the natives had come to a
halt on the bank, where one of them aimed his ancient
flintlock. Sweeney ducked just at the right moment and
the ball plumped harmlessly into the dirty water. It was
just as he had prayed. The natives couldn't swim. He was
going to make it!

He stopped short. Coming straight towards him was
little scow, propelled by half-naked rowers to either side
of the craft with its shaped dragon-head. And there on
the prow, like the devil himself, waited his executioner,

132

his scimitar gleaming in the sun's rays as he raised it for the only blow needed.

Bowing almost to the mosaic floor, the courtier advanced on the Lord of the White Elephant holding the round object in a bloody silken handkerchief. On both sides attendants held their breath in fearful awe; even the servant holding the punkah above the gold and ivory throne had ceased moving it. All eyes were set on the ruler.

The old man's papery hands with their claw-like nails were shaking with fury. His mouth was set and his wrinkled face was fixed in an expression of the most baleful kind. His eyes glittering and lethal, he watched the courtier advancing upon him with his gory bundle.

As etiquette demanded, the courtier's face was set in a smile, but inside he was quaking. He knew the ruler had already ordered the immediate execution of all Po's party for their failure to protect him. One wrong move on his part and it might well be his last. Forbidden by court protocol to look the Lord of the White Elephant directly in the face, he unrolled the bloody handkerchief and allowed its contents to roll onto the marble floor in front of his presence. Sweeney's head was revealed, and involuntarily the frightened courtier retreated a few steps, waiting for the outburst to come.

When it did, it was not directed at him, the bearer of the evidence that the murderer was white. Instead the ruler cried in his thin voice, '*Kill them . . . kill them*. Burn them . . . to death.' Then his head slumped on his chest with exhaustion, as if he too were dead.

WHOOSH! Like a gigantic torch the flame seared across the front of the forest in a vivid flash. Instantly the trees were burning and crackling merrily. As the greedy flames leapt high into the midday sky, they sent out a tremendous heat that made the watchers gasp for breath. Bold and the others stared at the conflagration aghast, already feeling the very air being dragged out of their lungs, as it advanced steadily on the Golden Pagoda – fanned by the wind that was now blowing.

There was another explosion to their right, as the unseen Burmese ignited a second pool of the 'fat that comes out of the earth'. Again angry flames leapt skywards and within a second, more of the forest was burning, the trees already beginning to splinter and tumble to the ground. The heat was so intense that the watchers began to back off, their faces contorted with horror at the sight of the wall of flame steadily advancing upon them. In the interior of the pagoda the horses scented the fire, tossing their heads from side to side, so that the troopers had to soothe and restrain them.

Desperately the waiting troopers under Ensign Hodgson looked at Bold. When would he give the order to attack? It would be far better to die wielding one's sabre on the enemy like a soldier than perish impotently in those terrible flames. But Major Bold seemed mesmerised by the flames, unable or unwilling to attack. Next to him the princess shivered, as if with the fever, as she drew the hem of her robe across her mouth for protection against the heat.

Bold's mind raced. Sweeney's trick had not paid off. Admittedly they had gained four or five hours before the yellow devils had set fire to the forest. Now they could either succumb to the flames or make one last desperate charge out of the Golden Pagoda. But it would be their last. The enemy outnumbered them ten to one. 'Men of the 41st Foot,' he commanded. 'will fix bayonets – *fix bayonets*!'

There was the slither of steel being withdrawn from scabbards, then the men held their long muskets awkwardly between their knees as they attached bayonets to muzzles.

Bold turned to his own squadron. 'Bold's Horse,' he ordered, 'will commence to walk at my command. Ready now.'

Ensign Hodgson, bare-headed with a bandage wrapped

around his forehead, raised his sabre to his lips in salute and cried, 'Bold's Horse at your orders, sir!'

Bold took one last look at them, as if he were trying to impress each man's features on his memory; as if he were seeing them for the last time. He told himself how brave and imperturbable they all looked, although they knew they were going to their deaths.

'Drummer boy!' he commanded.

'Sir!'

Bold looked down at the lad and swallowed hard. Poor little nipper, to die so young. Aloud he said, 'Drummer boy, beat the attack!'

The fresh-faced boy was obviously scared, but he raised his drumsticks and rattled off the call with a will.

Carried away by the danger, the movement and the rattle of the drum which had so often before signalled the call to battle, Riding Master Jones cried, 'Let's be having them, lads!'

'*Ay* . . . *let's have 'em!*' the cry rose from half a hundred British throats.

Bold could wait no longer. 'Death before dishonour!' he yelled in the battle cry of Bold's Horse and levelled his sabre in the direction of the enemy – already massing down below in their hundreds. 'ATTACK!'

They surged forward, kicking aside all remaining barricade's and urging their mounts down the steps; a great mass of angry men motivated by the primeval lust to kill, fear forgotten as they went to their last battle.

The Burmese below began to back off, some of them firing as they retreated in awe before the red-coated giants now advancing so purposefully. But Major John Bold at the head of his men, pistol in one hand, sabre in the other, took no pleasure in the sight of the enemy retreating. It wouldn't be long before their officers rallied them, and already he could hear the shrill trumpeting and heavy treat which heralded the arrival of the elephants bearing cannon in their howdahs. His horses would panic as soon as they appeared on the scene. No, they hadn't a chance. Soon the counter-attack would start.

With the first of the enemy barricades only yards away, the infantry pressed forward at the double, bent like men advancing against a heavy rainstorm. Bold's own men had already mounted and were beginning to force their way through the foot to lead the charge. All the while the drummer boy at Bold's side beat a furious tattoo, as if his life depended upon it.

The Burmese had rallied. They knew they had the matchless support of the elephant-cannon. Heads started to appear the length of the barricade. Muskets were thrust through the firing slots. Bold tensed for that first volley which would rip his front tank apart.

As the first elephant lumbered into sight, its gunners already aiming their cannon, there came a tremendous flash of lightning. John Bold was not fated to die yet. It was followed the next moment by the hiss of the retreating flames as the monsoon rain pelted down. But that was not all. Faintly, but distinctly, came the shrill foghorn from the delta. There was no mistaking it.

The soldiers stopped in their tracks, ignoring the rain which was already soaking their redcoats. They looked in wonder at the direction the signal had come from, almost as if they could not believe their own ears. It was there again. '*It's the* Diana . . .' they cried in sudden joy. '*The bloody old tea-kettle . . . The* Diana *. . . We're saved!*'

FOUR: BETRAYAL

1

Rangoon was virtually deserted now.

The great storm, the arrival of the *Diana*, and one day the rest of Campbell's fleet, had turned the tables completely. With his main army still far north on the Arracan frontier, the Lord of the White Elephant and the Golden Foot had apparently panicked. He had fled northwards with his court and at the same time had ordered the populace to follow him with their oxen and horses – while his troops had been ferried out of Rangoon by boat in the direction of the town of Ava. Now all that was left were a few peasants, unwilling or unable to flee, and the ruler's wounded soldiers who were hastily dispatched by Campbell's troops as soon as discovered. Brown or white, Campbell's soldiers had little mercy on the Burmese. They killed as easily and unfeelingly whenever they came across one of the helpless wretches, as they might do a dog.

Up at his headquarters in the battered, smoke-grimed Golden Pagoda, General Campbell had problems other than the fate of the Burmese wounded to occupy him. One week after the expeditionary force's arrival in the Burmese capital, the General explained his dilemma to his assembled officers with the aid of a crude map that one of his aides had drawn up on advice from the princess. With sweat running down his red face, the General pointed at the map and said, 'The last we heard of their ruler he was heading north some fifty miles from here. But he has left the Irrawaddy and gone onto the land. That indicates to me that he is not going to go much further. It is my opinion, gentlemen, that he intends to camp somewhere in that area and wait until the main army on the Arracan joins him.'

He let the words sink in and Colonel Cavendish, suddenly said, 'You think then, General, that this Lord of the White Foot or whatever the damned heathen is called, intends to attack us here in Rangoon?'

Campbell caught the note of fear and could scarcely conceal his contempt when he replied. 'Yes, I do, Colonel. We have already learned that he has not withdrawn his army completely from the area of Rangoon. Major Bold,' now Campbell smiled, 'will you be so kind as to report?'

Smartly Bold stepped into the centre of the big hall, while Cavendish eyed him, telling himself that this was the great hero who'd had the damned audacity to get half his A company killed – a company he had uniformed and armed with his own money. He took an instant dislike to the fellow and his damned darkies. Bold knew nothing of this. He was sorely tired and his mind was concentrating on his report. 'Sir,' he addressed the General and then his officers, 'gentlemen. On Wednesday last I was ordered to take a half squadron and sweep the area north of here. Apart from a few stragglers we found nothing of the enemy until we came to the villlage of Kemmendine,' he stumbled a little over the unfamiliar name and the princess standing shyly at the back of the assembly nodded encouragingly. 'It is on the banks of the river and is what the Burmese call a war-boat station. The terrain there is very swampy and wooded, making our approach difficult. But we managed to get close enough, using the bank of the Irrawaddy River to ascertain that the Burmese had erected the usual stockade there – and that it was strongly defended. Then we withdrew.'

Cavendish blew out his cheeks and said, 'I suppose you thought it wiser than attack, eh, Major?'

Bold stared at the Colonel and didn't like what he saw. Yet he answered politely enough. 'Sir, I was ordered to bring in intelligence, not fight a pitched battle.'

'Of course you were, of course,' General Campbell intervened hastily. The heat was bad for everyone's nerves. He didn't want any squabbling among his officers. That sort of thing led to bad blood and bad blood led to duels. He wanted none of that in his command. 'So we

140

can conclude from Major Bold's report,' he said, 'that our man has possibly armed a series of these fortified villages along the Irrawaddy, because he has guessed that we plan to advance north, and will be forced to use the river. Apart from Bold's horses, we have no mounts, mules, elephants or oxen to transport an army overland. So what do we conclude from this?' General Campbell answered his own question. 'The core of the resistance to us here in Burma is their ruler. Eliminate him and their resistance will probably crumble. At present, it seems, that their ruler is conveniently located not far from Rangoon – probably *here* at Ava, waiting for his army on the Arracan to return so that he can attack Rangoon. I conclude that even with one quarter of our present force here in the capital, we stand a good chance of capturing this fellow.'

There was a murmur of agreement among the officers present. Already the fever was beginning to attack their soldiers; for the climate in Rangoon was decidedly unhealthy, and they longed for some enterprise which might bring the war to a speedy end.

'But there is the problem of transport, sir,' someone objected.

'Exactly,' Campbell agreed and moped his streaming face once more. 'That's the bugbear of it all. But before I tell you what I intend to do, let me call that lady over there. She will tell us what she knows of Ava.' He beckoned to the princess.

Head bent, she came forward with that graceful shuffle particular to Burmese woman. She attracted all their eyes, including those of Colonel Cavendish, who told himself that she was the kind of filly, he wouldn't mind touching his spurs to.

'Now my dear,' General Campbell said softly, 'would you please tell my officers what you know of yon place.'

'Yes General Campbell,' she answered and still not raising her eyes, she commenced. She explained that Ava was located on the banks of the Irrawaddy, sited on the top of a cliff-like structure overlooking the great river. It had long been fortified along the waterfront with the usual teak stockade, which was armed with cannons. What calibre and how many she did not know, but she knew there were cannons there. Campbell nodded and said encouragingly, 'and what of the other side of the town facing the jungle, is that fortified as well?'

'No, General,' she answered softly. 'Because there is no road leading to Ava through the jungle and it is generally supposed the only attack would come from the Irrawaddy.' She looked up suddenly, and smiled sweetly at John Bold.

Cavendish noted the look: so that was the game was it? The young cavalaryman had already been at those delightful little bubbies which nudged through the thin silk of her blouse, had he? And probably all the rest of her, too. It would just serve the upstart right, if he also partook of this delectable piece. He licked his lips.

'I hope you noted what our young lady here just said, gentlemen?' Campbell was saying. 'The landward side of Ava is not defended, at least not by a stockade and cannon. So it must be there we attack.' He made the statement quite baldly, without any drama or pathos. But it caught his officers completely by surprise. Despite that oppressive heat, there was immediately an excited buzz of comment.

Campbell let them chatter for a while, then he raised his big hands for silence and said, 'Let me state this to you so that you will realise the full seriousness of our enterprise. Originally the Governor-General dispatched this expedition to punish the Burmese. Yesterday I received a message from him by packet from Calcutta to state that all is changed. Whitehall and the Horse Guards have ordered that far from merely punishing the Burmese, we shall wrest their kingdom from them for good. Burma, gentlemen, is to become part of our Empire.' Campbell drew himself very erect at the statement and some of the listening officers were so impressed that they snapped to attention as if the King himself had just made a proclamation. He went on, 'In the light of this decision from London – and Calcutta – it is imperative that we capture yon Lord of the White Elephant and the Golden Foot and make him submit to our will before he can be joined by his main army. Lop off the head and the plant will wither of its own accord. So how are we going to do it? Major Bold once more, please.'

Bold shook his head, as if he were finding it difficult to stay awake and stepped forward three paces to the crude map. He jabbed his forefinger at several spots along the Irrawaddy River. 'Here . . . here . . . and here! These are all fortified villages just as the one at Kemmendine, already described. They are designed to prevent us sailing up the river to Ava. But that is the only route we can take, because of our lack of transport. So how are we going to do it without fighting a pitched battle at each of these places?' He answered himself. 'Subterfuge, gentlemen.'

'How do you mean *subterfuge*, Major?' Cavendish barked. 'Please explain yourself, sir?'

Bold looked at him coldly. 'You have probably heard the sound of hammering which has been coming from the *Diana* these last two days, Colonel?'

'Can't say I have,' Cavendish replied, 'Well what of it?'

'This. The skipper of the *Diana* is currently heightening the sides of his ship with metal plate and also working on the rockets.'

'So?'

'So, he is preparing for a journey down river, Colonel.'

The others looked at Bold sharply and then at the General for his reaction. The latter nodded, as if he knew all about it. 'You mean the *Diana* is going to tackle the Irrawaddy?' a colonel of one of the sepoy regiments asked startled.

'Yessir'

'To what purpose?' the sepoy colonel snapped. 'After all that can only alarm this Lord of the White thing-a-bob chap. I can't see how the *Diana* can do much good.'

'Agreed, sir,' Bold answered promptly. 'But it is not the *Diana* with which we are concerned.' He looked at the General and the latter took over swiftly. He knew that these senior Colonels didn't like being lectured by a young Major nearly half their age.

'The *Diana* is being steel-plated to give more protection to the lascars who stoke her boiler and the rocket battery we are installing is to frighten, more than anything. As you know, gentlemen, the *Diana* is a bit of a seven-day wonder with the Burmese. They have never seen anything like her before. Wherever she goes, she attracts their attention. They can't fathom out how she can move without wind and sails.' He hesitated for a moment and then lowered his voice significantly, 'And that is exactly what we want – *to attract their attention*, while we slip another force past those river forts without their noticing. That is what Major Bold here meant by subterfuge.'

'You mean, sir,' Cavendish was the first to react, 'you are to send a force to Ava to seize their ruler?'

'Exactly. It is now or never. We have little time left, with the men falling sick all the time in this hell-hole. We need to have done with this matter swiftly. Now the plan is this, while the *Diana* draws their attention, our force will slip by unseen and when it arrives just south of Ava, it will disembark and attack from the landward side. I know it is not going to be easy, but it can and it *will* be done. I see no other way.'

'What will this force be made up of, sir?' the CO of the sepoy regiment who had spoken before asked eagerly. It was obvious that he wanted to be part of it. Campbell smiled to himself. He knew it was not duty, glory or patriotism that animated the man; it was the prospect of loot. The Colonel was an old India hand; he knew these native princes and kings always hauled vast fortunes around with them.

'I'm afraid I shall have to disappoint you, Hawkins,' he answered. 'Bold, here, will go of course, because he has his horses, but I think we need a battalion of British foot for the main storming party.' He looked at Cavendish, who had gone a little paler.' It means—'

At that moment the urgent rattle of the drums calling to quarters, and the shrill blare of the trumpets, followed

144

an instant later by the hollow boom of cannon, all cut into the General's words.

'What the devil is going on out there on the river?' half a dozen voices called at once, and in a flash they were all crowded at the far end where they could observe the shimmering water.

An amazing scene met their eyes. Coming down the stream on the ebb tide, bobbing up and down on the water, there was a score of little rafts. All of them burning fiercely. They were made of rows of bamboo to which were attached jars of gunpowder, cotton and other flammable objects.

'Fire rafts!' Campbell exclaimed. 'I haven't seen the like of yon since the Peninsula.'

'What's the object of them, sir?' someone queried.

'The same as when that pirate Drake singed the King of Spain's beard at Cadiz three centuries ago . . . Look how the tars have tumbled to what those yellow heathens are about!'

Indeed the sailors had swiftly realised what the unseen Burmese intended when they'd launched the rafts upstream. The enemy anticipated that one of the rafts would catch a ship's cable or her bow, lodge there and spread the flames up her wooden structure to the sails. Now the barefoot tars were thrusting the danger away from the sides of their vessels with grappling irons, cursing eloquently or shoving them towards the shore with their oars so that they could burn themselves out there harmlessly.

For a long ten minutes the assembled officers watched, some of them like Campbell praying fervently that none of the treacherous little fire rafts would get through; for they desperately needed all the shipping they could muster.

None of them did so. Then it was all over, and the sweating sailors were giving themselves three hearty cheers and their relieved Captains were ringing the brass ships' bells to indicate that the mainbrace would be spliced immediately as a reward for their efforts.

145

Campbell breathed again. 'Phew! That was a damned near thing. And it shows me that we are in danger here in Rangoon. They've obviously got this place under observation all the time. We shall have to take great care with our subterfuge.' He frowned, 'Colonel Cavendish, I am afraid I cannot use you on the expedition to Ava. I shall need my white artillery and foot here in the Golden Pagoda.'

Cavendish's relief was all too obvious, although he made a play of pulling a stern, manful face like one who feels he has been badly done to.

Campbell was not impressed. He turned to Colonel Hawkins of the native foot. 'It'll be your battalion after all, Hawkins,' he snapped.

'Thank you, sir,' Hawkins answered promptly with a big grin and Campbell told himself he was already calculating the amount of loot he might take at Ava.

Campbell continued as outside the tars cheered again as they lined up for their pannikin of grog. 'We must proceed with the utmost secrecy. The men must not be told where they are going. All provisioning for the expedition must be done, as if we are fitting out another patrol landwards. The *Diana* will be boarded at night, with horses muffled and the foot with their equipment similarly silenced. We must work on the assumption that the Burmese out there are watching us all the time and we must give them no opportunity to guess what we are about.'

Cavendish raised his hand like a schoolboy asking a question of his teacher.

'Yes, Colonel?' Campbell said. 'What about the – er – lady?' he indicated the princess, who had once more retired to the edge of the assembly.

'What about her?' Campbell countered.

'Well, sir, she may have been of some – er – use to some of us,' he looked pointedly at Bold. 'But she is a native, sir, and one of them. What do they say, eh? Blood is thicker than water.'

'And what do you suggest should be done with her?'

Campbell asked icily, while the princess stared pointedly at the floor and Bold's anger grew by the instant.

'Nothing very drastic, sir,' Cavendish replied easily. 'Only that she be placed in my headquarters' custody, where I shall be personally responsible for her conduct until the expedition returns from Ava.'

Bold opened his mouth to speak, but Campbell silenced him with a stern look. He said, 'Well, as both our headquarters will be located here in the Golden Pagoda and I may need the young lady to help with the language difficulties, I suppose that should be all right. Very well, Cavendish, she is your responsibility until we have their damned leader back here – in chains.'

'Yessir,' Cavendish smirked at Bold, 'I shall do my best to ensure she is well taken care of while she is at my HQ – *personally*'

Someone in the assembly sniggered knowingly and Cavendish made a great play of looking around with his eyeglass to find out who it was.

Thus the decisions were made which would bring death and dishonour to some, gain and glory to others. But within John Bold there lay a new bitterness.

2

The next twenty four hours passed swiftly.

While Campbell sent repeated patrols beyond the outskirts of Rangoon in an attempt to prevent spies observing
his preparations on the river, the little expedition was
prepared for the operation on the Irrawaddy. Each of the
troopers had to surrender a certain number of longboats
and sailors to man them to the required force, while the
skipper of the *Diana*, having completed the process of
adding armoured plate to his ship to protect his lascars,
now set about readying 'the mattress'. This being a series
of rockets banked one above the other on a wooden ramp.
When fired the whole mass of some fifty rockets at a time
would slam into the enemy positions.

'Of course,' as Campbell explained to a worn and over-
worked Major Bold – who was having two of the naval
longboats adapted to carry his troopers and their mounts
– 'those rockets won't do much damage. But they present
an impressive spectacle and will no doubt put the breeze
up the Burmese. At least long enough for your chaps to
slip by their post unseen.'

It had been decided that the expeditionary force would
attempt to pass the first fortified waterfront village of
Kemmendine during the hours of darkness, while the
Diana made the greatest possible noise and spectacle
there. As soon as that was accomplished, the *Diana* would
sail on, overtake the longboats and during night of the
next day would repeat the same tactics at the next village
of Puzendown – some twelve to fifteen miles further up
river.

'Naturally,' Campbell had pointed out, 'there is the
danger that the river might prove too shallow for the
Diana before she reaches the outskirts of Ava. Then you

will be entirely on your own, but we'll hope that eventuality does not take place, eh?'

Dutifully Bold had agreed, but he had not been altogether convinced. Indeed he wondered if it would be wise to sail the *Diana* within twenty miles of Ava, where the Lord of the White Elephant was supposed to be in residence. If he were to achieve surprise, he did not want the Burmese ruler even to suspect that the British force was so close.

Colonel Hawkins of the native foot agreed with him on that score. Hawkins, a tall officer in his late forties, dried-out and yellow-skinned from twenty years in the subcontinent, secretly hoped that this expedition would provide him with enough loot to retire to Shropshire and there become a nabob. He'd barked afterwards, 'It's all right for the General. His days of active soldiering are over. He just makes the plans. *We*,' he poked a finger at his narrow chest, 'have to carry those plans out and mind this, Major, there is many a slip between the cup and the lip.'

That same afternoon one of Cavendish's patrols brought in a strange-looking Burmese, who was obviously still high on *bhang*. He rolled his dark eyes and kept moving his shaven head crazily from side to side like an inmate of Bedlam. The sergeant in charge of the patrol explained how they'd bumped into a dozen Burmese who had charged the redcoats, without even drawing their swords from their scabbards, shrieking their heads off and some of them baring their chests as if challenging the startled redcoats to shoot. They'd been obliged readily enough and this one had been the only one to survive, thanks to the quick wits of the NCO who had felled him with a blow from his ramrod.

Campbell was interested and the princess was brought in to interpret, while the prisoner rolled his eyes and gibbered away like a man demented. As she made sense of the disjointed babblings that came in answer to the General's quetions, she said he appeared to be a member of the 'Invulnerables'.

'The Royal Invulnerables is their full name, sir. They

are the madmen and desperadoes of the ruler's Army. They are kept mad with *bhang* or opium, and told they are invulnerable. That nothing can stop them. Besides before they go into the attack, the most favourable circumstances for that attack are decided by the court astrologers.'

Campbell whistled softly through his teeth. 'Sounds like the Holy Writ to me – the Chaldean soothsayers tricking the Assyrian kings and all that. But please ask him how many of these savages are running wild out there.'

Dutifully the princess translated, but it took her several minutes of interrogation before she received any definite answer. 'There are about four thousand of them along whole length of the river between here and Ava. They appear to be roaming about in bands with no real control, looking for "wild foreigners", as they call you, to kill.' She broke off lamely and thought of John Bold, as if she had just realised he was one of the 'foreigners' they were aiming to kill.

Behind her Colonel Cavendish, who was keeping 'a tight watch on the minx – just in case,' as he'd explained to his fellow officers, told himself he was glad *he* was not sailing up the Irrawaddy this night. These 'Invulnerables' looked decidedly frightening.

Bold and Hawkins remained impassive as Campbell dismissed the native with a curt command to the NCO who had brought him in – 'shoot the beggar'. Hawkins cleared his throat noisely in the fashion of the Indians, something he had picked up over the years, 'they're just another lot of black buggers,' he commented. 'Shouldn't worry about them. My sepoys will soon show them off, sir.'

Campbell grinned. 'That's the style, Colonel. I thought you were going to ask me for more troops. Or do you want all that loot to yourself. Hawkins?

Hawkins had the decency to flush a little.

Campbell's smile vanished. 'Well, gentlemen,' he addressed Hawkins and Bold, an air of finality in his voice. '*Nomen es omen*,' as the dominie used to say when I was

150

a wee laddie at the Academy. The name is an omen. And with a couple of names like Bold and Hawkins, how can we fail, eh? At all events I have every confidence in you. You know your orders. I expect you back here within the month, Royal Invulnerables or not, bearing with you the Lord of the White Elephant.' His face hardened, 'or *his head*, if needs be.' He stiffened to attention and raised his right hand in salute.

Standing at the far edge of the crowd of officers, Riding Master Jones pulled a face and observed to no one in particular. 'Things must be bad, if the General salutes, that they must.'

But that night, after the troops had commenced embarking under cover of darkness, the officers stood on the quayside toasting the expedition with iced champagne. 'And not with John Company funds either, gentlemen,' Campbell proclaimed in high good humour once more, 'Highland Archie has paid every single bawby for this wine hissel.'

Standing a little way apart from the rest of the party, John Bold and the princess waited for the signal to go in sad silence. All the men called her that, and he didn't even know if she had another name. Both were preoccupied with their own thoughts. There was little they could say to each other, *openly*. Yet each felt if the other would only speak, it would release a flood of emotion that might never cease. So they waited almost mute, listening to the distracting thunder of the guns, as out in the delta the soldiers embarked.

Cavendish was saying to Hawkins, 'I envy you fellows, Colonel. The glory of it all.'

'Forget the glory, Colonel, give me the loot,' Hawkins, slightly drunk, chortled and the officers around laughed too.

It was the kind of animated, slightly unreal talk, Bold had heard more than half a dozen times before at moments like this. Then it had not affected him. Now it repelled him, as he realized he was leaving the princess behind with a fellow like Cavendish. She must have sensed his

151

thoughts, for her hand stole out and gripped his. 'Do not fear, John,' she whispered so that the others could not hear, 'I shall be all right. The General will look after me.'

'Of course,' he said, though without her confidence. The General had more on his mind than the safety of this foreign beauty. 'I shall return, you know,' he said softly. 'There is no doubt about that.'

She looked up at him and answered, 'I know you will . . . and I will still be here.

It was thus that Cavendish turned and caught them. His lips curled contemptuously. 'Yellow bitch,' he whispered to himself, slightly drunk now from the champagne, 'do your silly billing and cooing, now. But by God, when it's my turn . . . ' He didn't finish his sentence for the orderlies came hurrying towards their superiors to report that the longboats had loaded, while the General's aides ran back and forth, full of self-importance. It was time for the expedition to go.

With the *Diana* belching smoke in the lead, the little fleet was underway, the clatter of giant paddle wheels making the horses snort and toss their heads in fear, so that the troopers were kept busy soothing them and feeding them bits of cane sugar.

Standing at the bow of the longboat, Bold turned to stare at the land receding in the distance. For the first time in many years he felt that perhaps someone cared for him. Once again there was something to *live* for!

At four that morning, the *Diana* loomed up out of the low mist which now hung over the Irrawaddy, her boilers feathered and her paddle wheels momentarily motionless as she let the current take her to the first fortified village. The longboats started to group in a tight circle to her lee side, away from anyone who might be observing on land. One by one they positioned themselves, the oarsmen clinging to the ropes which had already been lowered from the side of the *Diana*. By a quarter past, John heard the click of the engine telegraph, as the skipper ordered his engineer to start the ship's engines once more and the *Diana* began to move the mile or so which separated them from Kemmendine. Already the gunners were fussing about their 'mattress', which would go into action immediately the Burmese spotted them and raised the alarm. That couldn't be long, John told himself, for the steady throb-throb of their engines carried a long way in the stillness of the night. Soon the trouble would start. Aloud, he said to Jones, who was the senior man in his boat beside himself, 'We'll be moving off any minute now. Stand by with the horses. Keep them muzzled.'

'Yessir,' Jones answered smartly and hissed out of the side of his mouth to the tense troopers. 'You heard the CO!'

Although they all expected it they were all startled when it happened. A flare hurtled into the night sky. *Crack!* It exploded directly above the *Diana* in a shower of silver stars. Almost immediately the steam ship was bathed in an eerie light. Bold heard the Captain, high above on the quarter deck, give the order: 'FIRE!'

The 'mattress' cracked into frenetic activity. Rocket after rocket hissed furiously into the sky, trailing a stream of red sparks behind. Clouds of thick dust rose everywhere. In an instant all was noise, chaos and sudden death.

The Burmese did not accept that tremendous bombardment tamely. Protected by their stout teak stockade, their gunners began to reply and grape, the size of large plums, howled across the water to clang on the *Diana*'s steel sides like heavy tropical rain on a tin roof. Cannonballs flung up huge mushrooms of whirling white water and up in the trees Burmese sharpshooters tried to pick off the men on the quarter deck, as more and more flares sailed into the sky above the steam ship.

'Cast off,' Bold said urgently.

'Aye, aye, sir,' the coxswain replied hastily and let go of the rope trailing down the side of the *Diana*. Everywhere other boats were doing the same. For all of them realized the importance of escaping into the outer circle of darkness beyond the light of the flares, before they were spotted by the embattled Burmese.

Their crews panting as the oars flashed in and out of the water, the longboats shot forward – ignoring the torrents of spray from the cannonballs falling all around the *Diana*. Once Bold thought they had been spotted when a flare exploded directly above the fleeing longboats, outlining them for what they were. Fortunately at that very instant, the *Diana*'s gunners let loose another salvo of rockets which rose with a banshee-like howl into the sky and then plunged down right on top of the fort – making the defenders dive for cover, and they rowed on unseen.

They had done it! The sweating rowers slumped over their oars in the inky darkness that surrounded the scene of battle. John Bold looked back and found a terrible beauty in the sight. For over the river there was a fantastic kaleidoscope pattern which took shape and died almost instantly thereafter like man-made forked lightning. Here and there a wayward rocket exploded close to the bank of the Irrawaddy and tossed up a ball of fire like a Roman candle; all the while the Burmese flares kept exploding over the *Diana* throwing her high, ugly superstructure into stark relief against the water.

John knew there was no time to rest. They had to push on, just in case the Burmese put out boats to tackle the *Diana* in that manner and discovered them by accident. He gave a soft order. All around their boat other commanders did the same. The weary sailors spat on their blistered palms and commenced rowing once more. Slowly, one by one, they disappeared into the darkness upriver. They had overcome their first obstacle successfully. Now they were moving into the unknown.

3

It was on the second day of the expedition up the River Irrawaddy that the *Diana* hit the sandbank. Immediately, the steady clatter of her big paddles became a furious, ineffectual churning and the ship's screws thrashed the muddy yellow water of the great river into a wild white. Still the steam ship stubbornly refused to budge from the sandbank concealed just below the river's surface.

After a while the Captain signalled John and Colonel Hawkins of the native foot to come aboard. Flushed and angry, he explained in his Welsh sing-song that he planned to attempt to reverse the ship, while the crews of the longboats would assist by towing her. And, he reminded the two army officers grimly, if they didn't succeed there could be 'a devil of a long wait' for the next tidal race to come up the river from the sea to flush out the trapped ship.

All afternoon the sweating sailors, assisted by the soldiers, toiled over their oars while the *Diana's* screws thrashed the water impotently time and again. She would not budge. At four o'clock, with the crews slumped in exhaustion, the *Diana's* Captain admitted defeat. 'What of the expedition now, gentlemen?' he put the question bluntly to the two officers.

Bold waited for Hawkins to speak; after all he was the senior man. The latter didn't hesitate and declared that they'd go on without the protection of the *Diana*. General Campbell's orders must still be carried out.

'Yessir,' John agreed promptly. 'If I may suggest, sir? We go as far as we can by water without discovery. Then we take to the land.'

Hawkins boomed, 'Exactly. Now then let's get cracking!'

And that was that. One hour later they were on their

way, with the stranded *Diana*, her skeleton crew now manning her cannon, disappearing rapidly round the next bend in the Irrawaddy. They rowed all night, glad of the coolness and well aware that they had to cover as much distance as possible before they were spotted. Once the teak forest on the left bank of the river opened up to reveal a village. But nothing stirred within as they passed it in utter silence save for the sound of their own breathing and the soft creak of the oars in the rowlocks.

Dawn came with the usual tropical suddenness. One minute it was dark and cool. The next, the sun was a fiery red ball on the horizon, bringing with it instant heat and the usual cacophony of jungle sounds. Now they could see the steaming green inferno into which they were steadily advancing without the armoured protection of the *Diana*. Once there was a tremendous splash and they caught a fleeting glimpse of a crocodile. As Sergeant Jones commented wrily sucking on his unlit clay pipe, 'Pray the Good Lord, we don't fall in, sir. Them creatures'd have yer down their gullets as quick as a dog's dinner.' As if to avoid the possibility, Colonel Hawkins decided the force should hide up for the day and get some rest.

The small tidal creek they pulled into was a beautiful place, surrounded by tall trees with emerald-green leaves. Yet its beauty palled for John once he realized he could smell pigs and the pungent fish-paste which the Burmese peasants used to flavour their rice. There must be a village in the vicinity. If he could smell it, it must be close and that worried him. As he told Colonel 'With your permission, sir,' he suggested to Colonel Hawkins, 'I vote we find the village and then set up a standing patrol to watch it until we are ready to leave again.'

'Excellent idea, Bold. Will you take your mounts?'

'No sir, they might give us away. I'll take one horse only for my riding master, Sergeant Jones. He can act as my galloper to you, sir, in case there's any trouble at the village.

Half an hour later the little patrol was on its way. The village turned out to be only half a mile away and they had no trouble finding it. It was the usual sort of Burmese fishing hamlet on the banks of the Irrawaddy: a collection of straw-roofed huts surrounded by a mangrove swamp. John whispered a command and his men settled down in the shade of the thick bamboo, three quarters of them falling asleep immediately while the rest kept guard.

By midday John had almost convinced himself that the village had presented no danger and that it would be safe to take the patrol back to the main body. But it was then that Jones nudged him in the ribs urgently and whispered, 'Sir, somebody's coming . . . into the village . . . from the other side, sir.'

Awake instantly, Bold could see that the villagers had stopped working on their fish. Instead they were staring intently to the north. Here and there, the half-naked women, up until now busy with their fires and cauldrons, were ushering their children fearfully into the huts. He didn't need a crystal ball to know that the humble villagers were afraid of the interlopers, whoever they may be. Hurriedly he raised his glass, carefully shading the lense with his hand so that it did not glint in the sun and reveal their position, and surveyed the first of the strangers now coming out of the mangroves. Half a dozen warriors mounted on shaggy ponies. On their heads they bore the conical helmets of the Burmese fighting man and their faces were heavily moustached. John could understand why the native women had hidden their children. Instinctively he guessed that these were the Lord of the White Elephant's élite – whom the princess had warned them about.

Next to him Jones read John's thoughts for he said, 'D'ye think they're looking for us, sir?'

Grimly, John nodded as he watched one of the horseman lash out at a cringing fisherman and bellow something at him. He was obviously asking a question. The fisherman shook his head hurriedly, as more and more of the warriors began to flood into the village, where they dismounted and swaggered up to the abandoned cooking pots. 'It looks, Jones, as if they'll stop here for a meal first,' John whispered. 'Then I bet they'll push on southwards, keeping close to the bank of the Irrawaddy. In due course, they'll spot our men; even if we rowed away now, they'd see the boats.'

Jones asked, 'What we'll do then, sir?'

'It's no use trying to dodge them,' John answered slowly. We'll have to deal with them while we have the advantage of surprise. Now this is what I want you to tell Colonel Hawkins . . . .'

At two o'clock precisely, with the sun at its zenith, Major Bold raised the carbine he was carrying and took careful aim. He had already long selected his target: an oafish-looking fellow, tall for a Burmese. But he did bear the golden umbrella, which indicated that he was their leader. Taking his time, John pressed the stock hard into his right shoulders and let the foresight cross the big fellow's face as he squatted there spooning up the rice, prawns and chicken of the frightened villagers. He felt not the slightest remorse for what he was about to do. The golden umbrella looked like a man who had taken what he wanted all his life, who had frightened and brutalized people. He deserved to die. He began to squeeze his trigger, while all around him his troopers did the same. In a moment all hell would break loose.

He took the final pressure and fired. The butt thudded painfully against his shoulder. There was a puff of black smoke which cleared almost immediately. For one moment John thought he had missed. The Burmese seemed perfectly all right. Then a stream of blood gushed from his open mouth and coloured the rice he'd just been enjoying. In that same instant Bold's troopers blasted off their own volley.

'It's them!' Hawkins yelled and raised his sword. 'Our chaps . . . No firing . . . '

Down the line of the ambush, the NCOs and officers repeated the order. 'It's them . . . *No firing!*'

A moment later the troopers came stumbling out of the forest, uniforms ripped to shreds by the thorns, with here and there a man limping or holding a blood-stained arm. They flung themselves down in the undergrowth with the waiting sepoys, as the noise of the approaching Burmese cavalry came ever closer. And as John Bold, his carbine gone now, came into view, Hawkins cupped his hands around his mouth and yelled urgently, 'Over here, Bold . . . Over here!'

How John Bold had managed to evade his enemy this long was beyond him. Now they were almost upon him. Running all out, he threw himself into the brush where Hawkins had concealed himself and lay there, choking for breath. Hawkins had prepared his ambush well, once Sergeant Jones had explained how matters lay with John. He had divided his battalion into two, placing two companies at each side of an extended V, the sepoys facing inwards to the teak forest through which the Burmese must come. The forest was not too dense to allow individual horsemen to proceed through it but the trees were too close to one another to permit a concentrated cavalry charge, which Hawkins reasoned might rattle his native foot. Now, if Bold's plan, worked, his sepoys would be able to pick off the horsemen individually – they had been trained in standard infantry musketry: a concerted volley every thirty seconds. Hawkins prayed they could pull it off. For if just one of the devils escaped, he would warn that Lord of the White Foot, or whatever he was called, that the expedition was on the way.

'There they are, Colonel!' John hissed excitedly.

A small group of horsemen were filtering through the teak a couple of hundred yards to the right, eyes fixed on the ground, obviously looking for tracks.

The bugler looked at the Colonel. Hawkins shook his head. 'Not yet,' he said, his voice controlled as he saw more and more of them were trickling through the trees straight into the centre of that killing V, unaware of the trap. Hawkins began to count them. When he had got up to two hundred, he decided that had to be the lot. Besides, a few yards more to the right and they would bump right into the two companies he had concealed there. He raised

159

his sword. Next to him his bugler pursed his lips around his mouthpiece. 'NOW!' Hawkins yelled fiercely and the signal was sounded.

The surprised horsemen hadn't a chance as both sides of the V erupted into fire. Men and horses went down everywhere and five minutes later it was all over for the dead and dying Burmese.

'*Cease fire!*' Hawkins cried, as if finally sickened by the massacre. Yet in the sudden silence he raised his voice again to order, 'Companies will advance – with bayonets fixed!' He said no more. The men would understand; they had done it before on other battlefields. There had to be no survivors.

John watched. He, too, had seen this sort of thing before often enough. It was typical of the callous cruelty of the Orient where life had little value. But he didn't like it. It was different when you killed a man in the heat of battle when your blood was roused. But this—. Then suddenly it happened. A group of sepoys had begun to search through a pile of still figures near to one of the few standing native horses, turning the bodies over with their boots, making sure that they were all dead, when a shot rang out. Before anyone could react, one of those they'd taken for dead had vaulted directly onto the back of the remaining horse, and then he was off. They had to watch him crouched low over the animal's flying mane, their bullets whistling harmlessly all about him. A moment later he had vanished. Next to a dismayed John, Hawkins groaned and said, 'Now the buggers'll know we're coming. . . .'

4

Cavendish crouched on the verandah, hardly daring to breath. She had not heard him, he was sure. But he could hear her and he salivated in excitement.

Cavendish had been drinking steadily since well before midnight. There had been claret with dinner in the mess. This had been followed by champagne and then when he had staggered off to his own quarters, he had ordered his servant to bring him a bottle of French brandy from his own private supply. That he had consumed, smoking cheroot after cheroot, all the while he had brooded about the woman they all called the princess, wondering what she would be like, stripping her mentally. By one that morning, drunk and aflame with desire, he had been unable to withstand the temptation any longer. Without a sound, he'd lowered himself over his own verandah on to hers some seven or eight feet below. Now as he crouched there, he peered into her bedroom through the open shutters. It was a hot stuffy night and she had thrown away her single sheet, so that her body was revealed in all its loveliness.

'By God,' he whispered to himself, 'what a peach!' His eyes took in the surprisingly full breasts, and he gloated. Like all native women she was shaven of pubic hair, and powdered, so that he could see everything. It was as if he were looking upon the body of one of those virginal kids they sold for five guineas a time behind the Vauxhall Gardens. The faint warning in the back of his mind which told him he was endangering his career was soon silenced. After all, he told himself drunkenly, she was only a nigger even if she did claim to be a princess.

He crossed to her bed on tiptoe without disturbing her. He wet his finger and placed it between her slightly parted legs. She stirred softly and gave a gentle sigh. He smiled to himself lecherously. The bitch liked it. They always did. What price Major Bold, the Hero of Rangoon, now!

She awoke with a start when he pressed his finger deeper into her, and also reached out to tug softly at one of her nipples. For a moment she was bewildered. Then she saw him bending over her, naked save for his shirt, and with both her hands she tried to remove his. But he held her easily, forcing his big finger even deeper into her, as she writhed to escape. 'Got some spirit after all, eh,' he hissed. 'I thought you'd niggers'd like it.' He went deeper, his breath coming in sharp, excited gasps. 'Like my wenches to have some fight in 'em. . . . Better in the end that way.'

'I shall scream!' she cried frightened by his brutal intensity. Then she said desperately, 'The General will hear of this.'

But Cavendish increased his efforts, grunting and enjoying himself now. 'The General's sick . . . with blackwater fever . . . pissing black again. I'm senior officer here in Rangoon now. My word is law.' With that he ripped his shirt over his head to reveal his own white body, devoid of muscle and hair, where the rigid red ugliness below was all too evident.

He laughed in her face, 'Didn't you know a stiff cock has no conscience. I bet you liked it with your fine Major Bold! Well, I'm here and he's far off in some damned jungle, probably rotting in his own dung already . . . so be silent and enjoy it!' He flung himself upon her with his full weight so that she felt his body engulf her, his hands everywhere, touching, prodding and feeling. Finally seized her plump buttocks and her knees, forcing them apart with his own. 'Now,' he gasped, 'this is going to be good . . . Spread 'em, wench. QUICK!'

She screamed.

In the rumpled, sweat-soaked bed, she lay weeping softly to herself. Her whole body felt defiled. Next to her he snored drunkenly, his organ flaccid now. He had taken her brutally, treating her worse than some cheap bazaar hoori. What would John think of her when he knew, that terrible thought crossed her mind time and time again.

What would he say when he learned just how Cavendish had defiled her? Would he even believe her? After all Cavendish was a fellow Englishman and officer. Would John believe that he had simply taken her without her will? Would he not think that she had given herself to the drunken monster of her own volition?

As she lay sobbing in the darkness, she knew that the white people would stick together and not believe her version. Yes, even John might think she had given herself of her own volition. She was doomed.

Just before dawn, Cavendish stopped snoring and began to turn in his sleep as if he would soon awake. And she knew what that meant. He would take her again. She stopped crying and stared out at the reddening horizon which heralded the new day and the disclosure of her shame. Her mood of despair had now been replaced by one of icy calm and resolve. Better she should act now than that John should return later and perhaps challenge Cavendish.

Silently and still completely naked, she slid from the rumpled bed, her mind made up. On the table there was the sharp-bladed knife she had used to peel her supper of – mangoes in what now seemed another world. Death in her eyes, she gripped it and crossed the room to where Cavendish lay on the bed, his sex fully exposed and defenceless.

She lifted the knife. It would have to be done with one swift slash. He must not be given a chance to move. Then he could bleed to death in a fitting punishment for the crime he had committed. Thereafter the English could do with her as they wished. She hoped they would kill her at once before John returned; she could not bear the shame of facing him. Slowly she started to bring the knife down.

Cavendish awoke with a start. He understood her intention at once and horror contorted his face. The yellow bitch was going to cut off his manhood! Instinctively he lashed out with his right foot. She yelped with pain as it caught her in the stomach. Unable to help herself, she staggered to the verandah. Half-crazed with shock, Cavendish went after her. Then she thrust the knife at him. He screamed as it slashed open his side and blood began to jet from the wound. For a moment he stood there staring at it as if he couldn't comprehend that this was happening to him. 'You whore . . . you murderous whore!' he gasped and lunged at her, trying to get the knife away from her.

She sprang to one side and slashed at him again. He groaned and felt the blade rip the length of his shoulder. 'You bitch!' he yelled at her, ignoring the urgent call from the sentry below.

He knew he had to silence her; sober again, he appreciated not only his own danger but also the scandal that would ensue if she lived to tell her tale. Not even his uncle in Calcutta, would be able to save him if she told Campbell what he had done to her. He caught her off guard and dived at her. The knife fell and she was slammed back against the verandah. For just a moment she balanced there, swaying wildly. Then she was over the edge and all that was left of her life were the few seconds until she hit the ground far below.

Weakly General Campbell hung on his servant's shoulder as the man held the tin chamber pot up for him to urinate into. Still his water was that black colour which was the symptom of the fever which racked his skinny frame. 'So ye say, the woman attacked ye, Colonel Cavendish,' he said and allowed himself to fall back onto his bed. Outside a sentry stood guard over the body, as if the princess might still prove dangerous in death.

'It was obvious she was out to kill me, General, 'Cavendish said, holding up his bandaged hand in proof. 'Probably she had been after one of us senior officers all along. You were lucky, sir, if I may say so, that it was not you – in your present state.'

At this moment, General Campbell told himself, it would actually be a relief to be dead. But he didn't tell Cavendish that.

Cavendish sneered, 'Perhaps it was part of her plot all along to worm herself into our good graces. How do we really know that she told us the truth about this Lord of the White Elephant, or that place Ava? She might have led our poor fellers directly into a trap.'

Campbell groaned weakly, and not only with the pain of his fever. He knew that if the expedition led by Hawkins failed to capture the Burmese ruler before his main army came down from the Arracan, he would be forced to evacuate Rangoon – even if it meant leaving the expedition behind to an uncertain fate. But at the back of his mind Campbell didn't quite believe Cavendish, though the woman had certainly wounded him. There was no doubt about that. The princess, as they had all called her, had not seemed the type to have murder in her. 'Are you quite certain that that was her intention?'

Cavendish elaborated: 'I shall bear the scars to prove it, sir, until my dying day. I woke in my room and found her bending over me, knife in hand. How I managed to escape her, I will never know.' He knew that 'Highland Archie' had no other course but to believe him. More than likely the old Scot was dying at this very moment and when he was dead Cavendish would really be the senior British officer in Rangoon. For a moment he indulged himself. 'The Victor of Rangoon' would look good as a headline in the *Old Thunderer*. Pater would be pleased and he could return to London in triumph, with his reputation made, rid of the damned Army for good.

Campbell looked, but he was suffering from a blinding headache. Miserably he said, 'I think I shall sleep again now, Cavendish.'

'Yessir,' the Colonel acknowledged eagerly, knowing that the matter was now dealt with, as he had anticipated. Campbell was in no position to investigate further. The campaign in Burma was in a state of crisis; Campbell would not want any trouble with the Governor-General on account of some Burmese whore; Cavendish had known that all along.

'See that she is buried today,' Campbell said weakly. 'I

wouldn't like the jackals to get at her body.' This time raised his voice. 'Orderly, bring the pisspot. I think I need to go again, dammnit!' 'Yessir, I'll see that the murderous bitch gets her six feet of earth this very morning,' Cavendish said smartly sa the batman came rushing in with the General's private thundermug at the ready.

Outside Cavendish stared up at the sky. He had done it! Within the hour the princess, as they used to call her, would be safely buried and by the time Major Bold got back to Rangoon – if he ever did – the matter would be long forgotten.

Colonel Cavendish felt a happy man. Once he had seen to the burial he would go over to the mess and have a glass of iced champagne. He felt he deserved it.

5

'If we had a bucket of this here weather', Sergeant Jones commented miserably, 'we could get a penny a' glass for it.' He shook his head and the raindrops tumbled from the brim of his shake.

Jones was right. The weather was terrible. Ever since the ambush forty-eight hours before, it had been raining solidly – turning the jungle trails bordering the Irrawaddy into a swamp and lashing the river itself into a fury, as well as soaking the men huddled together in the longboats.

John Bold reasoned that at least the monsoon did have the advantage of keeping the peasants inside their huts, so that they wouldn't spot the force sailing up the river – so he hoped. Now they were approaching the last phase of the operation and John hoped that even if the Lord of the White Elephant had been warned of their approach by the escaper, they still might be able to spring a surprise on him.

He nodded to Jones who had just reported to him and turned to Colonel Hawkins standing in the ankle-deep mud of the bank to announce, 'Well, all my horses are ashore now, sir.'

Hawkins nodded, 'It's going to be deuced dangerous, Bold. But if anyone can pull it off, I am sure you and your men can. Good luck to you.' Without giving him another glance, Hawkins then said to the sailor in charge of his boat, 'All right, Bosun, you can push off now.'

'Aye aye, sir.' The burly seaman nodded to his men and swiftly they propelled Hawkins' boat to the centre of the Irrawaddy where the other crafts waited in the rain. Minutes later the little fleet had disappeared into the gloom and Bold Horse's were alone.

Colonel Hawkins had not liked the plan one bit when John had first explained it. 'With the natives warned, there's little I'll be able to do against that stockade of theirs. All that would be possible is a feint. The real butcher business will be up to you and there can't be more than a hundred of you altogether.'

'One hundred and ten officers and troopers, sir,' John had said. 'But if we can achieve surprise by coming in from the land side while you feign an attack from the water, I feel we have a good chance of pulling it off. It really does all depend upon speed and surprise, sir.'

Finally Hawkins had conceded, 'Well, I suppose it's the only way . . . I'll do my best to give you the support you need.'

The next twenty-four hours passed in back-breaking monotony for John's dismounted troopers as they slogged through the mud and jungle on the bank of the Irrawaddy. Once or twice they found trails which led to Burmese villages that had apparently been abandoned once the soil of the area became worn out. But for the most part it was a hard slog through mangrove swamps, with the flanks of their horses lathered in black stinking mud.

Up front, Ensign Hodgson's troopers more than once had to use their sabres like the natives did their parangs to hack their way forward, and as a result of the thorny undergrowth there was nothing smart about Bold's Horse now. In the teak stretches, John was always afraid they would run into some of the native woodcutters, but fortunately their luck held. By the morning of the third day since parting with Hawkins' foot, John judged they were some ten miles south of Ava. Now he made his decision and while the men rested, he summoned Ensign Hodgson to him. 'You've done a good job, Ensign. Now you're going to have a break. I want you to take over command here.'

'And you, sir?'

'I want to do a reconnaissance of Ava. I am not going to attack blind. Once I know the lay-out of the place I shall co-ordinate our attack with Hawkins'.

With Sergeant Jones as his sole companion, John made good time throughout the morning, despite the rain. They caught their first glimpse of their objective around noon and immediately John could see that the princess had told the truth. Along the river the cliff which led up to the town was heavily fortified. The teak stockade running along it was of the kind they had become accustomed to in Burma. But this was more formidable than those of Rangoon. It consisted of some three miles of nine-foot high teak stakes, sharpened at the end and supported at regular intervals by earthen mounds on which cannons had been positioned. They were very ancient John estimated, noting their long barrels bound with copper supports, but they were vicious-looking things and quite capable of sweeping the length of the Irrawaddy at that point.

'Exceedingly formidable, sir,' Jones commented after John had lent him the glass to look at them.

John could not but agree and turned his attention on the town itself. It sprawled right across the plain behind its protective wall to the very edge of the jungle to the south. That pleased John. It meant he could bring his force up to the outskirts and still remain concealed before attacking. After that they would be completely exposed. For like most Burmese towns there were no trees lining the streets to offer shade – and cover. Instead there was the usual collection of straw-roofed wooden shacks, leading to the centre. Otherwise there was only a small stone pagoda and a hundred yards to its right, a more substantial building, also made of stone. Indeed this and the pagoda were the only stone buildings in the whole town. Obviously this was where their quarry was domiciled, both Jones and Bold concluded.

Through his raised spy glass, John recognized the kind of slate-covered brick structure that he had already seen a lot back in Rangoon, and the trellis windows were protected with rice paper instead of glass. He followed the street which ran from the house to the south and to the jungle in which they were currently hiding. At the moment it was thronged with priests in saffron-coloured robes as well as soldiers and traders hawking their wares.

But the crowd could not hide the fact that the dirt road was dead straight.

'Are you thinking the same as me, sir?' Jones queried.

John lowered his glass. 'And what *are* you thinking, Sergeant Jones?'

'Well, sir, cavalry could go up that road like shit through a goose – if you'll pardon my French, sir.'

'You're quite right,' John replied. 'With a bit of luck we could be up it, grab his nibs and be off back here with him before the devils know what's hit them.'

'My thoughts too, sir,'

'Leave a troop to protect the road where it enters the jungle to cover our retreat and leave another outside his domicile while we're attacking . . . ' John thought aloud, 'Yes, it could be done. But it would be nip-and-tuck and we'd have to go at it like merry hell.' He frowned, 'But we are forgetting those damned cannons yonder. If their gunners are smartish enough and we get held up, they could turn that stretch of road from the house into a veritable slaughter-house, Jones.'

'Colonel Hawkins and his footsloggers'll take care of them, sir,' Jones said encouragingly, and they left to find Colonel Hawkins and tell him what they'd discovered.' . . .

It was midnight of that same day. All the talk, the fears, the plans, the expressions of hope and good fortune were over. The time for action had approached and as always in battle, everything now depended on luck.

By this time Hawkins would have landed his soldiers downstream of the town and would be proceeding on foot towards the stockade, where he anticipated, the Burmese would have been warned and would be awaiting the assault. John had promised the infantry Colonel that he needed only an hour; thereafter Hawkins could start withdrawing his men to the boats. By that time – God willing – the Lord of the White Elephant would have been seized and John would be riding hell-for-leather to the agreed rendezvous on the Irrawaddy.

One hour before dawn Bold's Horse were in position, crouched in the jungle on both sides of the road which led to the house that must house the Burmese ruler. At dawn, or when it was just light enough to see, they would attack. Without being told, the troopers started to loosen their sabres in their scabbards and to test the locks of their pistols.

John turned to Ensign Hodgson who would lead the troop that was to cover this withdrawal, and whispered, 'How do you feel?'

'Nervous, sir,' the younger officer confessed. He laughed, 'Expect it's because I'm new to this game. And on account of my blood. We high yellers, sir, are supposed to be a bit windy at times like this.'

John peered at him as if seeing the Ensign for the first time. All along, he suddenly realized this man had been concerned about his mixed ancestry and what others thought about him. His heart went out to Hodgson for a moment. 'Listen, I fought at Waterloo when I was your age and at half a dozen other battles since, so I am a veteran campaigner. But I can tell you this I am *always* nervous. As for this high yeller stuff, discount it. A man's a man.

'Thank you, sir,' Hodgson replied.

There was no further time for reflection and the voice of Jones was heard, 'Tighten girths,' he ordered softly.

Obediently the troopers did so. No one wanted to lose his saddle during the wild charge to come; that would be fatal.

The next command came from John Bold himself, 'Mount up,' he ordered 'and mind, no noise in the ranks.' Even so, somebody's sabre jingled and Jones cursed the man angrily.

Saddle on his mount, John jerked at the bit to show he was in charge. Then drew his sabre and rested it on his right shoulder. His men did the same, making what seemed to him the devil of a row as the sharp blades came slithering out of their metal scabbards. He knew there was a note of finality about that sound. It meant the assault could not be long now.

A sudden crack. A hiss. A shrill whistle. As one, all their eyes looked to the sky above the river. There it was! A rocket shooting into the pre-dawn sky. It was the signal Hawkins' foot were going in to the attack.

As the first cries of alarm came from the river, there was the bass roar of a British infantry volley, which rolled and rolled down the valley of the Irrawaddy below the cliff. John's nervousness vanished in a flash. He was in complete control of himself. It was as if iced water coursed through his veins. Half-raised in his stirrups, he pointed his sabre in the direction of the town and cried above the snap-and-crackle of musketry, 'Bold's Horse will advance! At the trot – ADVANCE!'

His force dug in their spurs. Like a great moving wall of men and horseflesh, they moved down the street, rising and falling in unison in their saddles, sabres flashing blood-red in the sun's first rays.

Scarlet flame stabbed the shadows to their right. A trooper howled with sudden pain and slumped down over the mane of his horse, sabre tumbling from his grasp. Next to John, Ensign Hodgson jerked up his pistol and fired at the sniper in one and the same movement. He was rewarded by a kill.

More bloody work was to come. Half a dozen Burmese, armed with matchlocks ran into the street from a side road. A couple knelt and prepared to fire but John, the Ensign and Sergeant Jones were quicker off the mark. They'd fired as one and Jones yelled in triumph, 'Pick the bones outa those two.'

The four remaining Burmese dropped their weapons and fled. John knew they were doing all right so far. But once the locals brought their cannons to bear on Hawkins' infantry, he wouldn't last long. He'd be forced, as a result of the casualties, to retreat.

There was the clatter of further horse hooves. 'Prepare

to receive cavalry!' John yelled at his men. 'Native cavalry!' This was it.

A barbaric mob swung round the corner at a fast clip, mounted on shaggy native ponies and most of them armed with curved swords whilst carrying round brass shields. It was like a scene out of medieval history. Here and there, some of them bore ugly long lances, draped with animal skins. As one, they charged Bold's Horse.

There was an audible metallic thud as the two bodies of horse clashed. Within seconds there was a whirling mass of horsemen, jostling for position, shouting their heads off, cutting thrusting and standing up in their stirrups to level a blow at those who had already fallen from their terrified steeds.

'Cut through 'em!' John yelled time and again, as he thrust and parried, 'Cut through the buggers!'

He slashed at a Burmese who was trying to spear him, and the man went flying from his saddle, a gaping scarlet wound in the centre of his face. Another, already dismounted, grabbed at John's stirrups and tried to unseat him. Instinctively John lashed out with his steel-shod boot and his assailant went under, to be trampled to death.

The steam was going out of the Burmese cavalry's attack. By now they had lost cohesion completely and had broken up into small leaderless groups. They had stopped beating their drums, too, and were mulling around waving their weapons threateningly, but with little more heart for the attack.

'Break off!' John utilized the pause. 'At the trot . . . ' To Ensign Hodgson he yelled above the racket coming from the river bank. 'Keep your eye on them when we get inside the house, Ensign!'

'Yessir!' Hodgson yelled dutifully and levelled a tremendous swipe at one of the Burmese horsemen who had ventured too close.

As they came closer to the house, John could see a skirmish line hastily being formed outside under the command of a golden helmet. His heart leapt. That meant he had got the right place after all. Only a high official would

173

guard the ruler. Cruelly he dug his spurs and yelled at the top of his voice, 'Charge . . . Ride the swine down . . . CHARGE!'

His men surged after him, jostling and shoving for position. John flung himself from his horse, followed by Jones and a couple of troopers to clatter into the front hall – with Jones shouting, 'And no bloody stopping to loot either!'

A ball whistled by John's right shoulder as a shot rang out and marble splinters showered him from the nearest wall. Jones returned fire without aiming. Even so, the marksman came tumbling down the broad staircase and slumped with his neck broken, moaning softly. Jones kicked him just to make sure and cried, 'Which way, sir?'

For a moment John was lost for words. Above him there were intricately carved and gilded doorways, all inlaid with ivory and gems. Which one hid the Lord of the White Elephant?

It was Jones who reminded him. 'Where ye find his nibs' women, sir, ye'll find him. They're all like randy old goats.'

'Of course, the harem. Follow me!'

Now more and more troopers were streaming and skidding into the place. John charged up the stairs with his men after him, their spurs jingling. He flung open the first door, pistol at the ready. Peacocks came tumbling out in crazy, noisy profusion. Otherwise the room was empty. So was the next, and the next. But the bolts of silk, the furs and open ivory chests strewn all over indicated that someone was about to take hasty flight. John prayed that he was not already too late. Surely they had not made all this effort for nothing?

They clattered further down the long corridor in their heavy cavalry boots, the passage illuminated by the scarlet flames coming from the stockade. Hawkins wouldn't last long against that kind of bombardment, John told himself. *Christ, where was that damned Lord of the White Elephant?*

Two half-naked fat men in silk came waddling down the glowing passageway to meet them. Their plump sweating faces were hairless, their eyebrows had been plucked and their breasts bounced to and fro like those of a woman.

'Eunuchs!' Jones exclaimed and then he saw the silver axes they both bore. 'Christ, watch it, sir!' he bellowed in warning. 'Or they'll make you one of them—.

John parried the first Eunuch's blow. For a moment he feared he might drop his own weapon but he held on to launch a wild blow to the bulging, hairless stomach before him. The eunuch slammed back against the wall, a huge slash across his guts. Slowly he slithered to the floor trailing blood behind him. Meanwhile Jones had already fired his pistol at close range. The other eunuch was lifted clear off his feet as his face erupted into a bloody gore.

A moment later the two members of Bold's Horse had thrown open the door of the room which the eunuch had been trying to defend and stopped dead in their tracks. They had found the Lord of the White Elephant's harem!

6

'God Almighty,' Jones gasped as more and more troopers came running into the room only to skid to a startled halt, as they themselves had done, 'did ye ever see so much naked female flesh, sir! Cor, if it ain't an imperial knocking-shop!'

At any other time John would have laughed, but the minutes were running out fast. He stared hard at the couple of dozen women of all shapes, sizes and various colours who cowered in seeming terror at the far end of the room. Where was their quarry?

He saw that they all appeared to be clustered around a skinny woman who looked a bit taller than the average Burmese female. Something – afterwards he never knew what – told him to look at the woman's hands which clutched at the silken cloth she had thrown over her face. They formed veritable claws, wrinkled and with the nails unpainted John could not imagine that such an old wretch would do much for the ruler's flagging libido. Then he had it. The nails! Not only were they unpainted in contrast to those of the other women, they were also exceedingly long in the manner of high-caste Burmese who did no work. They indicated someone of great standing.

'Sergeant Jones,' he cried, very excited now. 'Seize that woman . . . the one in the middle!' Jones pushed his way through the sobbing women to grab the one in the centre. He snatched her veil away to reveal a face that John had already seen in what now seemed another age.

'Well, I'll go to our house,' Jones gasped, 'it's a frigging man.'

'No, not just a man,' John answered, 'It's his nibs himself . . . the Lord of the White Elephant and the Golden Foot!'

Thrusting and pushing, at times half-carrying the feeble

old ruler, John's party fought its way back downstairs to be greeted by the sound they'd been dreading all along. Without any mistaking, it was that of Hawkins' buglers sounding the retreat. The foot had had enough, no doubt having suffered all the casualties that Colonel Hawkins could bear to take. Hence his withdrawal to the boats . . . not much time was left.

Ensign Hodgson clattered across. Both he and his horse had been wounded, but all the same he managed, 'Why, sir, you got him!' as he saw John and one of the troopers flung the old man across the back of a riderless horse.

'Yes and I damn well hope we can keep him. Hawkins has just sounded the recall. We've got to get out of here smartish.' Even as he spoke he raised his pistol and shot yet another sniper who was crawling along the opposite roof to take aim at the troopers crowded below. Behind him there was another one waving his arms as if signalling to the gunners at the stockade. John fired again, but this time he missed and he couldn't afford to stop and reload to aim again. The gunners over there would see them soon enough, he reasoned.

'Start falling back, sir,' Hodgson yelled, 'I'll cover you with my troop.'

'Take no risks, Ensign!' John cried back, swinging himself into the saddle next to the horse carrying his unconscious booty. He slapped it over the rump and they began to move out, whilst over at the stockade the firing started to die away.

'Good luck, sir,' the Ensign called, touching his sabre to his lips in formal salute, white teeth gleaming, dark eyes flashing with excitement. As long as he lived John would remember him like that: alive, vital, full of that same youthful exuberance which *he* had lost on the field of Waterloo.

All his remaining troopers were moving down the road back to the cover of the jungle, each one tensed for the stockade's opening crash of cannonade. It came soon enough. They had gone a mere twenty yards when they heard the howl of the first ball. With a crash it struck the road to their front, bounced off its surface and sped on its way through the wall of one of the native huts.

'Damnation!' John cursed. They were already ranging in on the squadron.

He dug his spurs into his horse's flanks, holding on to the reins of the other with his free hand. Again the cannon thundered. This time the native gunners were using grape. It came hissing and singing down the length of the street. In an instant half a dozen of his troopers were on the ground, as if scythed from their saddles by an invisible reaper. A horse panicked and tore down the street, bearing its dead rider with it. Yet they pushed on, until they were just some two hundred yards from the protection of the jungle. Already John had lost ten of his men.

Ahead loomed crossroads, where they would have no cover to protect whatsoever. Just beforehand, he held up his hand urgently and cried 'Halt!' Vaulting from his saddle, and flinging the reins of both his horses to Jones, he crouched low and approached the danger spot. Taking off his shako, he balanced it on the end of his sabre and cautiously thrust the weapon round the corner.

The enemy reaction was immediate. A burst of grape came spluttering down the road, some of it chained together so that it would have ripped apart anybody in its path. His sabre sang as a ball struck it and he felt an electric shock run straight up his arm. The cunning Burmese gunners had zeroed in on the crossroads. He withdrew his riddled shako and threw it into the dust, shaking with frustration. For the time being well and truly stalled.

The problems behind them were mounting, too. Ensign Hodgson's men covering their rear were steadily being forced back. Little groups of native cavalry constantly rushed them, their confidence returned now that they had the superior numbers, and Hodgson was suffering casualties all the while.

John realized that the odds against them were high. They were being forced into a trap where there were less than a hundred of them, faced with perhaps thousands of the enemy, steadily being compressed into an area of a few hundred square yards. Soon the enemy sharpshooters would be picking them off one by one at their leisure, and in complete safety. *God, how was he going to get his men out of this one?'*

As if answering his inner cry of desperation, Ensign Hodgson came galloping up, forcing his mount through the carnage of battle. He waved his broken sabre, and cried something which John could not understand. But the survivors of his troop did. They broke off the latest skirmish with the Burmese lancers and followed their officer, carried away by the crazy logic of battle.

'NO!' John shrieked, for it had dawned on him what Hodgson was going to do. *'Don't do it, man!'*

Too late. The Ensign's doomed band of horsemen clattered by him and charged down the crossroads, crying out like men demented. For just a moment John thought they might make it. The native gunners were busy sponging and reloading their guns, brought down from the nearest earthern mound to cover the crossroads. They were recocking their locks and by some miracle they might not do it in time. That was not to be.

Against a background of drumming hooves that seemed to fill the whole world, John could only watch aghast as he waited for the inevitable.

The guns crashed like the knell of doom. A great cloud of thick black smoke rose instantly. For a moment the riders vanished into it and then it cleared, John groaned aloud at the appalling carnage. The road was packed from side to side with the dead and dying, animals and men. And they included the young Ensign, lying flat on his back, still clutching what was left of his sabre. John did not need to be told that he was dead. For the blow which had felled him and his mount had ripped off both his legs at the knee. John turned away, sickened by the sight.

Next to him Jones said softly, 'A brave young man, sir.' John could not answer. For a few moments he was paralysed by emotion and indecision. There was nothing more he could do. They were doomed – and that was that. Then he realized his duty to his remaining men.

They depended upon him. 'Sergeant Jones,' he heard himself say.

'Sir!'

'Do you think you could manage to get what's left of us across?'

'Yessir, but what do you intend?'

'Try to take a small party across first. Once they have opened up, you follow with our prisoner and the main party – at the double!'

'But that's suicide, sir,' Jones objected. 'You're using yourself as a human target. You'll get your head blown off while we make a dash for it as they reload.'

'Exactly,' John answered quite calmly.

Jones stared at him. 'But that's not right, sir. Let me do it. I've had my days. With all due respect, sir, you're a young man,' he hesitated momentarily for he had seen John with the Burmese woman back in Rangoon, 'well, you've got something to live for. Me, all I've got is rum and whores.'

For a moment John did think of the princess and then dismissed the vision as quickly as it had come. He was in charge. It was his duty to do his best for his men. 'Do as you're told, Jones,' he snapped harshly.

'But sir—'

'No buts! I am your commander. It's my decision and my responsibility. You'll do as I say. Are you ready now?' John tugged at his reins.

It was then that the miracle happened. A shrill whistle came from the direction of the river and for a moment it drowned the noise of cannon-fire and musketry. There it was again, only much louder and closer this time. There was a strange churning sound, too. Hurriedly he curbed his horse. In the same moment that he did so, there was the banshee-like howl of massed rockets shooting into the sky, before they came crashing down right onto the Burmese batteries.

Sergeant Jones looked at his CO, tears of relief and gratitude in his eyes, 'We're saved, sir' he choked. ' . . . *it's the Diana, sir . . . SAVED!*'

Envoi

'Our hearts are sick of fruitless homing
And crying after lost desire.
Hearten us onward! As with fire . . .'

RUPERT BROOKE

'I'm awfully sorry, Bold, my boy,' the General said shakily. General Campbell was still recovering from his bout of blackwater fever and was very weak. His face had become even gaunter and there was an unhealthy greenish colour to his skin. 'But I'm afraid you'll have to accept the dreadful fact that your – er princess *did* attempt to murder Colonel Cavendish while he slept.'

John fought to control himself. His nerves were ragged as it was, and he was almost at the end of his tether. Three days before they had spent a murderous twelve hours in the teak forest pursued by the Burmese, before they'd been able to rejoin Hawkins in the boats under the protection of the *Diana* once more.

Even the river journey had not been without its dangers and strain. Twice they had been attacked in force and it had been a close thing before they had been able to beat off the enemy. By the time they had reached Rangoon to be welcomed by the cheers of Campbell's staff officers – for news of their imperial captive had preceded them – John had felt totally drained. But he had not been allowed to rest. After the congratulations, the back-slapping and the voices telling him what a splendid fellow he was, he had been summoned to the General's sick quarters in the Golden Pagoda. Here Campbell had congratulated him, too, and assured him that Lord Amherst would be informed of his 'sterling work'. For now it was almost certain that the Lord of the White Elephant would make peace with the East India Company and Amherst intended to demand Burma's four northern provinces, including the Arracan, from him – perhaps the whole of Burma. The Lord of the White Elephant would never threaten British India again! And Burma would become another jewel in the Imperial crown.

John had listened, not really interested. His mind was on the princess, for he had not been able to spot her among the crowd cheering on the quay, nor had he seen her here in the Golden Pagoda. Once he knew she was safe and well, he would sleep the sleep of the just, right round the clock. For his eyelids were like lead weights. But the General's next statement had driven all thought of sleep right out of his mind. Campbell had been too bluff an old soldier, too used to death and ordering men to die, to soften the blow. He had stated simply and clearly what had become of the princess.

John tried to be rational, but his heart bled and there was a swelling in his throat that made it difficult to swallow. 'But why, sir?' he managed to ask. 'She was on our side and had helped us. *Why* should she attempt to take Colonel Cavendish's life?'

Campbell shrugged weakly. 'That question I have been asking myself ever since Cavendish reported the death to me, lad. I know no more than ye.'

Then perhaps I should talk to Colonel Cavendish about it, sir. I think I can get *satisfaction* from him, if you will allow me?'

Campbell looked up sharply. He had understood what the young man implied. 'There will be no duelling between officers in my command, Major,' he said, then his voice softened again. 'Besides it is not possible, even if I were to allow it. Cavendish returned to Calcutta by packet twenty-four hours ago. He is leaving the Army.'

Campbell was glad that Cavendish had used his relationship with the Governor-General to have him recalled. Obviously he had anticipated Bold's reaction to the death of the woman everyone assumed was his sweetheart. But he just said, 'There was intelligence from London that his father is on his death-bed. Cavendish is to take his seat in the Lords. His regiment is to be sold to the highest bidder on the Horse Guards.' There was a note of bitterness in his voice now. 'Probably there is some perfumed popinjay in London who's never smelled gunpowder in his whole life putting a bid in for the regiment already.

My God, why can't the Old Duke put an end to such a foolish system? It's ruining the Army'

John was not interested in the future of Cavendish's regiment of foot. He knew he was exiled to India for good; the Old Duke, as Campbell called him, had told him that to his face back at Waterloo. With no hope in his voice he said, 'And what now, sir?'

Campbell looked at him hard. 'John, laddie,' he said. 'People like you and me – without money – can only make a career in the Army through our own efforts. There's no Cavendish cash backing us.'

'Yessir,' John said. But what did a career matter to him? All he could hope for, now, was that a bullet or a fever put an end to it all.

'But I'll tell ye this, John. You are not a conventional soldier and ye'll never make your fame or fortune in a conventional way. So forget your woes, laddie.' Suddenly he lowered his voice, 'I want to ask you to join the great game.'

'*The great game?*' John was intrigued in spite of his misery.

'Yes, my boy. The John Company has about reached the extent of what it can expand in India without risking trouble with the Russkies. For as we move northwards towards Afghani country and Persia, they are moving southwards. A strange game is being played out up there on the roof of the world, as they call it in Calcutta – a dangerous game. We have sent out some of our best officers, the bravest and most intelligent. Years later either they come back half-mad – or they don't come back at all.' He looked significantly at John, who felt a faint stirring of interest.

Anything was better than going back to the stifling routine of peacetime mess life and the barracks square. Besides hadn't General Campbell just said that this so-called 'great game' was dangerous? Perhaps he could meet a fine end out there on the 'roof of the world'?

Stiffly the General rose to his feet, and pointed to the big map of the subcontinent pinned to the wall. 'The

North-West Frontier, John. Kindly look at it ca
All that white indicating we know hardly a thing
it. But we *do* know that the tribes are massing and,
importantly, that the Russkies are behind it.' He
fronted John, 'We need a man like you up there. Will ye
go? For the sake of your country – and your career.
England needs its bravest and best there, and you're one
of the bravest and best I know.' He suddenly looked very
old and instinctively John knew the General did not have
long to live.

John Bold did not answer immediately. Instead he
thought of Lieutenant Sweeney, who had died because he
had wanted loot to provide for his old age . . . of Ensign
Hodgson spending his life so recklessly to purge the taint
of his mixed blood . . . of the princess and all the rest
who had died in this remote place. What did the people
back home know or care of their sacrifice? Had they all
died simply to fill the coffers of the like of Lord Cavendish, and allow him and his ilk to die of old age in soft
London beds? Was that what this empire-building and
'the great game' was all about?

The old General seemed to sense what was going
through John's mind, for he said softly, 'What else is
there left for you, laddie? You have no alternative . . . So
you have to go, haven't you?'

Slowly, John Bold's back stiffened like that of the veteran soldier that he was. Of course, he had no alternative.
For him there was no past, only the uncertain future, as
violent and unpredictable as the burning sun that could
be seen dominating the sky. 'I'll go, sir,' he declared, his
voice firm, all doubts vanquished. 'What are my
orders . . . ?'